Writing Great Fiction:
Storytelling Tips and Techniques

James Hynes, M.F.A.

THE
GREAT
COURSES

PUBLISHED BY:

THE GREAT COURSES
Corporate Headquarters
4840 Westfields Boulevard, Suite 500
Chantilly, Virginia 20151-2299
Phone: 1-800-832-2412
Fax: 703-378-3819
www.thegreatcourses.com

James Hynes, M.F.A.
Novelist and Writing Instructor

Professor James Hynes is a working novelist who has taught creative writing as a visiting professor at the University of Iowa Writers' Workshop, the University of Michigan, The University of Texas, Miami University, and Grinnell College. He earned a Bachelor of Arts degree in Philosophy from the University of Michigan in 1977 and a Master of Fine Arts degree from the Iowa Writers' Workshop in 1989.

Professor Hynes is the author of four novels: *Next*, which received the 2011 Believer Book Award from *Believer* magazine; *Kings of Infinite Space*, a *Washington Post* best book for 2004; *The Lecturer's Tale*; and *The Wild Colonial Boy*, which received the Adult Literature Award from the Friends of American Writers and was a *New York Times* Notable Book for 1990. His novella collection *Publish and Perish: Three Tales of Tenure and Terror* was a *Publishers Weekly* Best Book of 1997 and appeared on several critics' best-of-the-year lists.

Professor Hynes has received numerous literary grants and teaching fellowships. He received a James Michener Fellowship from the University of Iowa (1989–1990), and he was a member of the Michigan Society of Fellows at the University of Michigan (1991–1994). He received a Teaching-Writing Fellowship from the Iowa Writers' Workshop at the University of Iowa (1988–1999) and a Michigan Council for the Arts writer's grant (1984). As an undergraduate, he received the Hopwood Short Fiction Award from the University of Michigan (1976).

Professor Hynes is also a media and literary critic. He is a former television critic for *Mother Jones*, *The Michigan Voice*, and *In These Times*. His book reviews and literary essays have appeared in *The New York Times*, *The Washington Post*, *Boston Review*, *Salon*, and other publications.

Professor Hynes lives in Austin, Texas, the main setting of his novel *Next*, and is currently working on a new novel. ■

Table of Contents

Table of Contents

Table of Contents

Writing Great Fiction:
Storytelling Tips and Techniques

Scope:

We all think we have a novel in us, and in this course of 24 lectures, a professional novelist will guide you through a survey of the most important concepts and techniques behind the creation of contemporary prose fiction, using examples from a wide range of classic novels and stories, as well as some demonstrations of his own process. By taking you step by step through such topics as creating characters, composing dialogue, crafting plots, and using different points of view, this course will help you get that book out of your head and heart and into the hands of readers.

Lecture 1 considers how to prepare yourself, both logistically and emotionally, for beginning to write a piece of fiction, and Lecture 2 explores the concept of evocation, or the art of making fictional characters in a fictional world come alive, which is fundamental to most fiction.

The next four lectures provide an introduction to the creation of fictional characters. In Lecture 3, we explore the differences between fictional characters and real people and consider how a "person" who is only a few thousand words on a page can come to life in the mind of the reader. Lecture 4 shows how you can create credible and interesting characters by combining your imagination with observations of real people. Lecture 5 looks at several ways of introducing a character into a narrative for the first time, and Lecture 6 examines different types of characters, such as round and flat characters and major and minor characters, and explores how they work together in a story or novel.

The next two lectures are about writing dialogue. Lecture 7 explains the mechanics and grammar of dialogue, including tips on when and when not to use dialogue tags and adverbs. Lecture 8 is about using dialogue to evoke character and tell a story and about integrating dialogue seamlessly into the rest of the narrative.

Next comes the longest block of lectures in the course, six lectures about plot. Lecture 9 introduces the subject by discussing the difference between a story and a plot and by showing three ways to structure a traditional plot. Lecture 10 demonstrates how traditional plots can usually be diagrammed with the well-known Freytag pyramid, while Lecture 11 suggests ways you can rearrange or adapt the individual pieces of a traditional chronology to make your plot more complex and intriguing. Lecture 12 covers how to structure a narrative when you're not interested in using a traditional plot; Lecture 13 introduces techniques for getting a plot started; and Lecture 14 explores ways to bring a plot to a satisfying conclusion.

The next three lectures discuss the concept of point of view in fiction. Lecture 15 surveys the range of points of view, from the godlike, omniscient third person to the intimacy of the first person. Lecture 16 looks at the various ways you can use the first-person point of view, and Lecture 17 runs through the many varieties of the third person.

The remaining seven lectures look at a variety of individual topics of importance to fiction writers. Lecture 18 discusses the various ways setting and place can be used in fiction, while Lecture 19 explores pacing and the need to pace different types of narratives in different ways. Lecture 20 considers how to craft an individual scene, which is one of the basic building blocks of fiction, and Lecture 21 looks at the advantages and disadvantages of composing manuscripts in complete drafts. In Lecture 22, we'll take a look at the essential process of revision and rewriting, while Lecture

23 considers two approaches to doing research for a work of fiction. The final lecture touches on the changing nature of the publishing business and offers personal insights into the challenges and joys of making a life as a fiction writer. ∎

Starting the Writing Process
Lecture 1

Whether you're a beginner starting your first story ever or a professional with many publications behind you, few things make a writer more anxious than facing a blank page. One approach to overcoming this obstacle is to think about what the opening of a story is supposed to do: draw readers in and capture their curiosity. The beginning should also suggest something important about the story—the main characters, the tone, or the setting. But even if you know the story you want to tell, how do you decide what the first paragraph or sentence should be? In this lecture, we'll look at some ways to make the beginning seem less foreboding.

Three Questions

- One way to sneak up on the start of your story is to break the question "How shall I begin?" into three separate questions: the artistic question, the logistical question, and the psychological question.

- Simply put, the artistic question is: What is this story about? What's the idea you want to explore? You may have an entire plot worked out in your head already, or you may have only a character or a situation in mind. Whatever it is, something has motivated you to write.

- The logistical question relates to the technical aspects of starting a story, the basic decisions you have to make at the start even if you don't know everything about your story. This is actually a number of questions combined, such as: Who's telling the story? What verb tense will you use? What voice is the story in? These early choices can be daunting because every decision you make will have consequences later on, many of which you can't foresee.

- Finally, the psychological question relates to how you gear up—emotionally—to begin. Even published writers become anxious about starting something new. Trying to leap that psychological hurdle involves being able to answer the first two questions, at least in part. That, in turn, ratchets up the anxiety, because there's so much you could worry about in advance that it's a wonder anyone ever starts at all.

The Five Ws

- Another way to approach starting a work of fiction is by using the old-fashioned five Ws of journalism: who, what, where, when, and why. Assuming you have a rough idea of what you want to write about, try to give a brief answer to each of these questions pertaining to the story you want to tell.

- The first question to address is: Who are your characters, and how are they related to each other? The who question also encompasses the choice of point of view, that is: Who is your protagonist, and who is your narrator? Sometimes these two are the same person, but that's not always the case. Often, the story is told by a third-person narrator, who can vary from the godlike, seeing into each character's thoughts, to one who is more like a surveillance camera, relating what the characters do without revealing their inner lives.

- The answer to the who question determines, in large part, how you answer the next question: What happens in the story? Another interpretation of this question is: What is your story about? Do you have some larger theme you want to get across, or are you just telling a good tale? Even if it's the latter, you still have to think about another version of the what question: What effect do you want the story to have on the reader?

- The where question seems relatively simple at first glance: Where is the story set? But this question leads to a more complex one: How important is the setting of the story to the story itself? In answering the where question, you decide whether your story is tied to a specific geographical and historical context and whether it is, in part, about that place and time or whether it is more archetypal and timeless.

- The question of when the story takes place is also more complex than it seems at first. It can identify the historical time of the story or the time it takes place in the lives of the characters. It also asks: When is the story being told in relation to when it happened? Is it being narrated in the present tense or in the past tense by a present-day narrator? If you tell a story in the past tense, you gain the benefit of hindsight, but if you tell it in the present tense, what you lose in hindsight you may gain in immediacy and suspense.

    o   Other aspects of the when question include: At what point in the story does the plot begin, and how do you order the events of the plot? Do you tell the story chronologically, backward, or moving backward and forward in time?

    o   Answering this question is at the heart of learning how to construct a plot, because you come to realize that the same series of chronological events can be told in many different ways. By deciding what to reveal and when, you're choosing the most important moments in the plot.

- Finally, the why question asks: Why do the characters do what they do? What do the characters want, and why are they in the situation of the story? Is it a situation of their own making, or is it a situation that has been thrust upon them? Of course, asking why the characters do what they do is both the hardest and the most essential question you must answer. Indeed, for many writers, trying to answer this question is the reason they write novels or stories to begin with.

A Simple Story?

- To illustrate how the answers to these questions might help you get started, let's take a simple story as an example. Let's say we have a married couple, Sarah and Brad. One Friday night, they decide to take in a baseball game, but during the middle of the game, Sarah tells Brad that she's unhappy in the marriage and wants a divorce.

- On the face of it, this seems to be a simple story; we started with two characters and a specific setting, and we told what happened in chronological order. But as soon as Sarah says that she wants a divorce, the story becomes more complicated than it seemed at first. It turns out to have started before the "beginning," and it sets up a complex dynamic between the two characters.

- A couple of lessons can be learned from this example. One is that a story is not mere chronology. In fact, we might say that most stores are not chronologies but rely on backstories. In his famous series of lectures about fiction writing, *Aspects of the Novel*, the British novelist E. M. Forster made a distinction between story and plot. Story, according to Forster, is the chronological listing of events; plot is the story plus causality and motivation.

- Another way of looking at this idea is to consider that all stories begin *in medias res*, "in the middle of things." Even stories that seem to begin at the very beginning, such as the opening of the book of Genesis, actually begin in the middle. Although it may seem as if we can't get much closer to the beginning than "in the beginning," even this opening presumes a previously existing character—God.

- This leads to a larger philosophical point about fiction: Literature is the creation of order out chaos and the creation of meaning out of meaninglessness. Stories may feel natural, but they don't occur in nature. As writers, we imagine a series of events or we borrow them from life, we order them in a certain way, we choose to highlight some facts and ignore others, and we bring these events and characters to a conclusion or a resolution.

- The fact that even a simple-seeming story can suddenly turn complicated brings us back to the difficulty of deciding where to begin. We know the basic facts about Sarah and Brad, but to explore this situation, we must start making choices—about what's important to tell, what's not, whose point of view to tell it from, and when in the story to begin.

- Even if you've decided on the answers to the five Ws, you still have to think of the first words of the story. Do you open with a description that sets the scene, an exchange of dialogue, an interior monologue, some action, or a combination of these? One possible solution is to outline the story in advance, but many writers prefer to improvise as they work.

This approach allows you to discover the story in much the same way that a reader does.

Psychological Question Revisited

- It's clear that starting a story involves making a number of choices, and that, in turn, can ratchet up a writer's anxiety. Let's return, then, to the psychological question mentioned earlier: How do you gear up—emotionally—to begin? One way to sneak up on this question is to remind yourself of what you don't need to do or know to start a story.

- First of all, writing a story is not necessarily linear; you don't have to write it the way the reader will read it. Writing can be more like putting a puzzle together: You can start anywhere in the story; then, when the larger picture gets clearer, you can craft a beginning.

© Stockbyte/Thinkstock.

A whole novel might be developed by answering the five Ws about a couple at a baseball game, working backward and forward in the characters' lives.

- You also don't have to know how the story ends. Sometimes knowing the ending is a good thing because it gives you a point to aim at, but sometimes not knowing can allow you to discover where the story itself wants to go along the way.

- Further, you don't have to have an outline, and even if you do, you don't have to stick to it. Be prepared for happy accidents.

- Your story doesn't even have to be good to begin with. As a writer, you have the luxury of being able to do as many drafts of a story as it takes to get it right, or you can revise as you go along. Don't be afraid to start over or go back and fix something, no matter where you are in the process.

- Finally, keep in mind that creative writing isn't a science. The only rule in this endeavor is: Whatever works. Throughout these lectures, we'll look at many choices for presenting stories; the best way you can use the lectures is to adapt the possibilities in these choices to your own work, taking whatever is useful and ignoring the rest.

Suggested Reading

Forster, *Aspects of the Novel*.

Writing Exercise

1. Without thinking too hard about it, try to recall a vivid image you may have seen recently, in real life or on television, and see if you can imagine a story to explain it. You can start with the Faulkner technique: Simply describe the image, such as a mother yelling at her child in the supermarket, then branch off from there, explaining why the mother is so exasperated or why the child is being so difficult. Then try Fitzgerald's technique with the same image: Outline the life of the mother so far—her girlhood, her courtship, the birth of her child—and work up to the moment in the supermarket. See which approach works best for you.

Building Fictional Worlds through Evocation
Lecture 2

One of the most venerable tropes in the teaching of creative writing is this: Show, don't tell. But what exactly does this dictum mean? When teachers of creative writing invoke it, they often mean that a scene or story was under-dramatized or that the writing trafficked in vague generalities. For example, a writer might tell us something that is generally true about a character without fixing that trait or action in a specific moment or situation. In this lecture, we'll see how showing rather than telling can make your writing more immediate, vivid, detailed, and visceral. We'll see how it invites readers to identify with your characters and participate in the story, if only in their imaginations.

Telling versus Showing

- Let's consider two versions of a scene, one that gets the facts across and one that puts the reader in the scene with the characters. Here's the first version:

> I was driving home from work this afternoon when some jerk came out of a side street and cut right in front of me. I was angry about something my boss had said that afternoon, so instead of just letting it go, I sounded my horn and tailgated the guy for half a mile. He pulled over, and we nearly got into a fight.

- Now let's look at an excerpt from what a fiction writer might do with this same scene:

> Naturally, as I was just about to cross the river, a guy in a Jeep Cherokee with enormous tires shot out right in front of me and cut me off. Worse yet, he was a young guy, with big redneck sideburns and a feed cap, and when I honked my horn, he gave me the finger and a big nasty grin. Worst of all, he had out-of-

state plates and an NRA bumper sticker, and all of these, along with my rage at my boss, made me erupt.

- Note that the outline of the two versions is the same, but the second version has much more detail. Instead of "a guy shot out in front of me," it's a young guy with sideburns and a baseball cap. He not only cuts the narrator off, but he seems to enjoy it. It's essentially the same story, but the second version is fleshed out with many more details about the two characters and the setting. The reader is much closer to being in the mind of the narrator.

- When creative writing teachers say, "Show, don't tell," they mean: Give us more detail, make it dramatic, and put the reader in the scene.
  - o Writing fiction by showing rather than telling means bypassing the logical, analytical mind and going for the gut, engaging the readers' senses, not just their minds. More important, you're engaging the readers' imaginations and allowing them to fill in the gaps by drawing on their own experience.

  - o What you're doing, in fact, is evoking the experience for the reader. The idea of evocation is at the heart of all fiction; it's the thing that allows a fictional story and imaginary characters to lodge themselves ineradicably in the minds of readers.

Defining *Evocation*
- The variants of the word *evoke* come from the Latin *evocare*, which means "to call out" in several different senses: to summon the spirits of the dead, to call forth a deity, or simply to summon another person. In English, when talking specifically about art and literature, the dictionary definition of *evocative* is "tending by artistic imaginative means to *re-create* ... especially in such a manner as to produce a compelling impression of reality."

- In English, *evoke*, *evocative*, and *evocation* can also mean "calling out or calling forth," "summoning a spirit by incantation," "calling up an emotional response," or "calling up memories, recollections, or associations." All these meanings apply when it comes to writing fiction because all these definitions have in common the idea of drawing something out of a reader's imagination, not just putting something into it.

- When you tell readers something, you appeal mainly to the rational, analytical mind, not to the senses. But when you show readers something, you draw out something that is already present—memories or imaginings—even if your readers don't know it. In other words, when you tell readers something, you make them witnesses, but when you show them something, you make them participants.

- Evocation is both a subtle and a powerful technique. It entails both the writer and the reader using their imaginations.
    o Writers use their skill with words to call forth scenes from their imaginations in enough detail that readers, without really thinking about it, use their own imaginations and memories to fill in the gaps. In the process, memories, emotions, and sensory impressions are evoked.

    o One of the benefits of evocation is that even though readers are doing half the work, they don't realize it, and they actually enjoy the experience. The feeling of being in the scene with the characters and being engaged by the narrative is one of the great pleasures of reading fiction. A phrase that brilliantly captures this effect comes from the American novelist and creative writing teacher John Gardner, who once defined fiction as the creation of "a vivid and continuous dream."

    o In her book *Writing Fiction*, another creative writing teacher, Janet Burroway, said that reading fiction allows us to feel strong emotions "without paying for them." This is what evocation is all about. When you get the reader to laugh, you're evoking merriment; when you get the reader to sweat and turn on all the lights, you're evoking fear. You don't just allow readers to visualize themselves in certain situations, but you prompt them to engage with the situation emotionally in the same way they would if they were actually experiencing it in real life.

The Balance of Detail and Economy

- Stephen King's *'Salem's Lot* is one of the best horror novels ever written. Here's a passage from it in which King evokes the arrival of spring in New England:

  > By mid-May, the sun rises out of the morning's haze with authority and potency, and standing on your top step at seven in the morning with your dinner bucket in your hand, you know that the dew will be melted off the grass by eight and that the dust on the back roads will hang depthless and still in the hot air for five minutes after a car's passage; and that by one in the afternoon it will be up to ninety-five on the third floor of the mill and the sweat will roll off your arms like oil and stick your shirt to your back in a widening patch and it might as well be July. (pp. 192–193)

By evoking memories we all have of heat and dust, an author can draw us out of our own lives and into the life of a laborer in another time and place.

- This passage is a wonderful example of how evocation works because it gives us a nice balance between detail and economy. As we've said, evocative writing provides significant detail, but it doesn't overwhelm the reader. The point is to draw something out of your readers, which you can't do if you pour too much in.

- This is a tricky balance to get right, and beginning writers often have the most difficulty with it. Just as one common error among young writers is not providing enough detail, another common error is to overcompensate by telling too much. Often, inexperienced writers will go on for several paragraphs about the appearance of a character or a place when a few well-chosen sentences or words would have done just as well.

- What are the right details to include? One way to answer that question is to include too much detail in your early drafts. Write much more than you need, then pare it back later.

  o You can also ask yourself some questions about the details you provide: Does this detail tell something that the reader didn't already know? Does it advance the story? Does it say something about the character that is specific to this scene?

  o Think about whether your details are concrete and appeal directly to the senses. Don't just write, "He was in love with her"; instead, write, "He felt his face get hot when she came into the room."

- Another issue to consider in making a passage evocative is the language itself. There are no rules in creative writing, but on the whole, evocation works best when you use active, specific verbs and avoid adverbs unless they're absolutely necessary.

  o Inexperienced writers often write such sentences as "She hurried quickly across the room" or "He pounded the table angrily." In these examples, the adverbs are unnecessary; it's clear from the verbs that she's moving quickly or that he is angry.

  o In most cases, use the strongest verbs you can think of. "It was raining" is not as evocative as "The rain hammered the roof and spattered the windows like buckshot." Instead of starting with the bland pronoun *it* and the even blander verb *was*, the second sentence makes the rain itself the subject; the strong verb *hammered* evokes not only an image but a sound and renders any adverbs superfluous.

Telling, Not Showing

- Despite the importance of evocation in fiction, it's also sometimes acceptable—even preferable—to tell a story rather than to show it. Many of the great books of the 18th and 19th centuries used telling as their default mode, as do many philosophical and satirical novels.

- In most conventional narratives, where much of the story is shown or evoked, there are also long passages in which the writer or narrator simply addresses the readers, telling them what they need to know. Just as a composer might vary the tempo of a piece of music to maintain the listener's interest, the fiction writer should provide variety among intensely evocative scenes, passages of pure exposition, and scenes that combine the two.

- In science fiction and fantasy, for example, there is often a passage or even an entire chapter early in the narrative known as the *info dump*, whereby the author takes a few pages to simply explain the world of the story before the action starts. Many fine literary novels and dramatic popular novels also have passages in which the author simply tells readers about the action or the characters.

- Another excellent example of a careful balance between telling and showing is Irène Némirovsky's *Suite Française*, a novel about the Nazi occupation of France during World War II. The book effectively combines exquisitely evocative passages with straightforward expository descriptions, making a point to present characters only as vividly as the reader needs to see them to advance the story.

Suggested Reading

Burroway, *Writing Fiction*.

Gardner, *The Art of Fiction*.

King, *'Salem's Lot*.

Némirovsky, *Suite Française*.

1. Try this exercise from John Gardner's *The Art of Fiction*: Write a passage describing a building, a landscape, or an object, but imagine that you're writing from the point of view of a parent whose child has just died. Describe the object without mentioning the child or death. The idea is to see if you can evoke a feeling of loss and grief in the reader without mentioning the emotions themselves.

How Characters Are Different from People
Lecture 3

One of the curious facts about the emotional life of human beings is that some of the most memorable and influential people in our lives have never existed at all. Odysseus, King Arthur, Jane Eyre, Mrs. Dalloway, Holden Caulfield—these imaginary people have become part of the common cultural currency of humankind; further, they are the very foundation of the craft of fiction. We often hear people talk about the difference between character-driven stories and plot-driven stories, but the fact is that every narrative begins with its characters. In this lecture, we'll explore the fundamental differences between the imaginary characters of fiction and the people we know in real life.

Characters in Fiction and Life

- Writers love to talk about how complex and layered their characters are—and they often are—but one major difference between fictional characters and real people is that characters are simpler.

    o A fictional character is constructed out of a few thousand words by a single writer, whereas a real person, even an uncomplicated one, is the product of millennia of heredity, centuries of culture, and a lifetime of experience. The best a fictional character can do is suggest a real person, not replicate one. They have only the illusion of complexity.

    o Indeed, their very simplicity is what makes fictional characters so vivid, because we can, by the end of a book or a play, see a fictional character whole in a way that we can't with most real people, even the ones we know intimately. But again, this wholeness is an illusion. In *Hamlet*, for example, we see only a few days in Hamlet's life, and even in larger-scale works, we never see as much of a character as we could a real person.

- Another difference between fictional characters and real people is that characters are made up of only the most dramatic or the most representative moments of their lives. We all live through moments of drama that might make for good stories, but the vast majority of our lives is made up of an endless chain of ordinary moments. Such moments are of no interest to anyone else and sometimes not even to us.

o When we write stories, however, we leave out all the ordinary, boring parts. The story of Hamlet starts when he learns, from his father's ghost, that his father was murdered by his uncle and his mother so that his uncle could be king. The rest of the play is about how Hamlet deals with this information, and by the final scene, he's managed to kill, or cause to be killed, everyone he thinks has wronged him.

o By contrast, a version of *Hamlet* that reproduced every single moment of his life would be both impractical and tedious. The life of a real person goes on and on, with no scene breaks or dramatic structure, but in a narrative, we see only the significant moments.

o Of course, some books try to reproduce the minute-by-minute progression of everyday life. The high-modernist novels *Ulysses* and *Mrs. Dalloway* both take place over a single day—and not a particularly dramatic one—in the lives of the main characters. But even with these seemingly all-inclusive narratives, we see only a few hours of the characters' lives, not a complete record of every moment from dawn to dusk.

• We know the people in our lives by what they look like, what they say, what they do, and what other people tell us about them—that is, by report. When we add this fourth way of knowing, we can expand our experience of real people beyond personal relationships to include all the real people we've ever heard about, from a friend of a friend to a movie star to a figure from history.

o Both the people we know personally and those we know about by report are equally real, and because of that, people in both groups share a certain impenetrable mystery: We can't know what they're thinking. We have no direct access to the consciousness of other living people.

- To understand this idea, consider the fleeting and digressive nature of your own inner life. Then, consider how impossible it would be to express that inner life to another person. Remember, too, that every other person in the world is experiencing the same kind of inner life, all the time. You quickly realize that each of us is alone in the universe inside our heads, surrounded by many other universes with which we can communicate only indirectly.

- Thus, the most important difference between fictional characters and real people is that the author can, if he or she chooses, let us know exactly what a fictional character is thinking or feeling. We can know fictional characters in the way we know ourselves. In fiction, we have direct access to the consciousness of other human beings in a way we cannot in real life.

Qualifications and a Paradox

- We must note three significant qualifications about this unusual intimacy we share with fictional characters, starting with the fact that it is an illusion. It's not real intimacy because the character sharing his or her innermost thoughts with us isn't a real person. The second qualification is that what feels like direct access to another consciousness isn't direct at all but is mediated through the talent, craft, and imagination of the writer.

- Taken together, these two qualifications leave us with a paradox: We know fictional characters only by report, yet through the genius of certain authors, we feel as if we know some characters even better than we know those with whom we have intimate relationships.

Through the special relationship that fiction can have with its characters, we as readers can have the sort of intimacy with these fictional people that we otherwise have only with ourselves.

o Even though your brother, for example, is real and infinitely more complex than such a character as Virginia Woolf's Mrs. Dalloway, if you were asked at any given moment what your brother might be thinking, you could only guess. But you can know with absolute certainty what Clarissa Dalloway is thinking at any given point in the novel.

o This paradox is at the core of the power of fiction to thrill and move us. In reading a book, all we really get are the imaginary thoughts of an imaginary person, but we feel as if we get something real and immediate, something we would never otherwise see: namely, the world through someone else's eyes, unmediated.

o The intimacy we share with fictional characters is only an illusion of intimacy, but it's such a powerful illusion that, at its best and most sublime, the book in our hands disappears, the voice of the author disappears, the world around us disappears, and we become fully engaged in the fictional world—at one with the character.

• The third qualification is this: Even though all writers could put us in the heads of their characters, not all of them do. The amount of access a writer allows us to have to the mind of a character varies on a continuum from complete intimacy to no intimacy at all. Most fiction falls somewhere in the middle, where most of what we learn about a character is through action and dialogue, with occasional access to his or her thoughts.

The Continuum of Intimacy
• Let's look at three examples of different points on the continuum of intimacy, beginning with *Mrs. Dalloway* on the most intimate end. This novel gives us one day in the life of Clarissa Dalloway, an upper-middle-class woman living in London in the years right after the end of World War I.

- Published in 1925, *Mrs. Dalloway* is written in a style called *stream of consciousness*. With this technique, the narration keeps close to the consciousness of its characters, shifting among perceptions, thoughts, and memories effortlessly and with lightning speed in an attempt to evoke the quicksilver nature of human consciousness.

- The novel relates the thoughts of Mrs. Dalloway at the very moment she thinks them in a way that's simply not possible for an outside observer to do in real life. Even if we knew Mrs. Dalloway and could ask what she was thinking, the mere act of translating her thoughts into speech would change what was happening; she would no longer be alone in her own mind but talking to another person.

- Another remarkable book published in 1925 is F. Scott Fitzgerald's *The Great Gatsby*. This book is narrated in the first person by Nick Carraway, but even though Nick speaks directly to the reader in his own voice, the narration here is less intimate than it is in *Mrs. Dalloway*.
  - We learn about Nick's history and his moral character through his narration, but we get the impression that he is holding certain things back.

  - Nick stands somewhere in the middle of the literary continuum between complete intimacy and no intimacy. We learn only what he chooses to tell us, which means that we learn no more about him than we might learn from him in real life.

- A third example is *The Maltese Falcon*, Dashiell Hammett's classic detective story, published in 1930. Hammett's main character, the private detective Sam Spade, appears in every scene in the book, and we see the entire story from Spade's point of view.
  - We get detailed descriptions of Spade's appearance, gestures, and actions; we also get a great deal of dialogue, in much of which Spade isn't necessarily telling the truth. But what we never get in the novel is direct access to what Spade is thinking,

and because *The Maltese Falcon* is written in the third person, Spade does not directly address us. Everything we know about Sam Spade we learn from observing him move and listening to him talk, the same way we would in real life.

o   At the end of the book, Spade must decide what do with Brigid O'Shaughnessy, the femme fatale who murdered his partner, but with whom Spade may or may not have fallen in love. It's an extreme situation, but Hammett doesn't plunge us into Spade's thoughts or allow his character to speak directly to us; instead, he lets us listen to a scene in which Spade thinks out loud about his feelings for Brigid and the choice he must make.

o   The scene is a vivid portrayal of a man wrestling with a bad situation. Although we don't have access to Spade's thoughts, we do have access to the dark world in which he lives. Hammett may not choose to show us every fleeting shift of Spade's consciousness, but he understands Spade and his moral universe every bit as deeply as Woolf understands Clarissa Dalloway's or as Fitzgerald understands Nick's.

Suggested Reading

Fitzgerald, *The Great Gatsby*.

Forster, *Aspects of the Novel*.

Hammett, *The Maltese Falcon*.

Woolf, *Mrs. Dalloway*.

1. Try to rewrite the scene of Mrs. Dalloway walking down Bond Street in the first-person style of *The Great Gatsby* or, perhaps, in the terse and more literal-minded approach of Dashiell Hammett. In other words, see if it's possible to evoke Mrs. Dalloway by having her tell us what she's thinking directly or by simply describing what she does or says as she moves through the scene. Conversely, see if it's possible to apply Virginia Woolf's stream-of-consciousness technique to Sam Spade's hard-boiled world and still keep the scene tense, energetic, and suspenseful.

Fictional Characters, Imagined and Observed
Lecture 4

All writers draw, both consciously and unconsciously, on behaviors and traits we have seen in ourselves or others, with the result that all the characters you create combine to form a portrait of your view of human nature. But although the roots of any character lie in your observations of yourself and of other people, those observations are refracted through your imagination. In the last lecture, we talked about the continuum between complete intimacy with a character and no intimacy at all, and in this lecture, we'll look at three other continuums: between observation and imagination, between exterior and interior approaches, and between psychology and circumstances in creating characters.

The Continuum of Imagination

- Some writers hew more closely to observation than to imagination, basing their characters almost entirely on people they know. Others write convincingly about characters or experiences they've never had themselves. Some writers even create characters who are a different gender, age, background, ethnicity, or temperament from themselves.

- Of course, there many variations along this continuum between pure observation and pure imagination. In historical novels, for example, the novelist may combine a real figure from history with both real and imaginary characters from the same period.

- Whichever pole a writer tends toward—observation or imagination—no writer relies purely on one or the other. Although some writers may base their characters on real historical figures or close family and friends, all must exercise their imaginations to the extent of seeing the world through the eyes of these characters and relating how the characters behave in fictional situations in which their real-life models may never have found themselves.

The Exterior-Interior Continuum

- The exterior-interior continuum relates to creating a character from the outside in versus creating a character from the inside out.
    - As mentioned in the last lecture, one of the defining features of fiction is that authors can give us direct access to the thoughts of their characters, even if they sometimes choose not to. But even for those characters whose thoughts we do have access to, there are many different ways to express them.

    - If you think of the continuum between observation and imagination as one axis, consider that there is another axis at right angles to this one, and the poles of that axis are the exterior approach and the interior approach.

- To help understand this idea, consider the difference between the British and American styles of acting as they were practiced during the 1950s and 1960s.
    - During this time, the method style of acting became popular among young American actors; this approach required the actor to identify with the character he or she was playing, to analyze that character's psychology in depth, and to use elements from the actor's own memories to evoke the emotions the character felt. In contrast, British actors at the time were trained to build characters out of small physical details and bits of behavior: an accent, a gesture, a prosthetic nose.

    - In this analogy, the American actor is using the interior method, building a character from the inside out, while the British actor is using the exterior method, building the character from the outside in. Fiction writers often use similar exterior or interior approaches.

Comparing *Emma* and *Jane Eyre*

- In the opening pages of her great comic novel *Emma*, Jane Austen lays the title character bare simply by telling us point blank almost everything we need to know about her: "Emma Woodhouse, handsome, clever, and rich, with a comfortable home and happy disposition, seemed to unite some of the best blessings of existence; and had lived nearly twenty-one years in the world with very little to vex or distress her."

- o After two paragraphs that explain Emma's family situation, Austen then tells us: "The real evils indeed of Emma's situation were the power of having rather too much her own way, and a disposition to think a little too well of herself; these were the disadvantages which threatened to alloy her many enjoyments. The danger, however, was at present so unperceived, that they did not by any means rank as misfortunes with her."

- o The rest of the novel is essentially a gloss on the first two pages, showing Emma's impetuosity, vanity, and cluelessness as she tries to manage the love lives of everyone around her without recognizing her own true love. There's no need for any *Mrs. Dalloway*–style intimacy with Emma's stream of consciousness, and there's no watching her slowly reveal herself through her speech and behavior. Austen simply tells us about Emma's character right from the start, then launches into her story.

- o Austen's description of Emma is frank, to the point, and unironic in the sense that Austen never has Emma do anything later in the book that undercuts her original description. Thus, with Emma fixed firmly in our imaginations as a vain, beautiful, meddlesome girl after reading only the first two pages, we are free to enjoy her effect on the lives of the people around her.

- o This approach works especially well with comic fiction, which often depends on types rather than fully developed characters or at least on characters who never really change our first impression of them.

- We can compare Austen's approach with a more indirect, interior one from the opening paragraphs of Charlotte Brontë's *Jane Eyre*. Again, in just a few paragraphs, we meet an adult, first-person narrator who is looking back with bitter irony on her unhappy childhood. We learn that she grew up in a household where she was considered an outsider, but she knew how to stick up for herself.

- The difference between Jane Eyre and Emma is that we don't learn everything we need to know about Jane in the first few paragraphs. Instead, we are drawn only gradually into the story while being given hints of her struggles to come.

- This technique works better than Austen's would in this instance because *Jane Eyre* is a darker, more serious book. There's more at stake here than romances and marriages among the idle rich; in the first few paragraphs of Brontë's book, we get the first hint of Jane's struggle to survive in a world in which she has no money, no connections, and no prospects.

- How you decide to configure characters—from the outside in or the inside out—has a profound effect on the sort of story you end up writing; the cause and effect here are inextricably intertwined.

  - A comedy, for example, often announces itself right from the start by being funny and staying funny, which requires characters who can be quickly and easily identified. In contrast, a drama often draws the reader in with an intriguing situation, the distinctive voice of a strong character, and the suggestion of more trouble to come.

  - Jane Eyre's world is more complex and more unpredictable than Emma's, and this extra complexity requires a more subtle and complex main character. Although Emma eventually grows up and learns not to meddle in the affairs of others, she doesn't do much to surprise us. But Jane, having shown us that she's smart and judgmental from the first page, turns out to be surprisingly wrong in her judgments of some of the other characters, particularly Mr. Rochester.

- Another way to look at the difference between these two approaches is to consider how much you want the reader to identify with the character. By writing in the third person and by telling readers directly of Emma's vanity, Austen invites readers to detach themselves from the character.

But Brontë has Jane Eyre address readers directly, inviting us to view the world through her eyes and to endorse her judgments.

The Psychology-Circumstances Continuum

- To understand the exterior-interior continuum from a slightly different angle, think about the difference between a character who is defined by psychology versus one who is defined by circumstances.

  o We're tempted to think that Emma is determined by her circumstances, but notice that it's the way her particular psychology butts up against the people and the world around her that makes the book funny.

  o In *Jane Eyre*, even though we have instant access to Jane's mind from the first sentence, it's the circumstances of her life that largely determine the course of the novel, even though we see that struggle mainly through its effect on her thoughts and feelings.

© Valueline/Hulton Collection/Thinkstock.

The books of American realist writers tend to be large-scale portraits of a whole city or class of people, emphasizing the social world through which the characters move rather than their individuality.

- Another tempting generalization is that character-driven narratives, such as *Mrs. Dalloway*, rely more on psychology than plot-driven narratives, such as *The Maltese Falcon*, but that's not entirely true either. Even though we don't have direct access to Sam Spade's mind and even though *The Maltese Falcon* is packed with dramatic incidents, the narrative mainly works as a record of his decisions. Underlying all his actions are thoughts that drive those actions, even if they are not directly expressed to the reader.

- Among the characters who are largely determined by their circumstances we might include many of the characters in Dickens, as well as those in the works of realist American writers, such as Theodore Dreiser, Edith Wharton, and Sinclair Lewis. Even though we have direct access to the thoughts of many of these characters, their thoughts are not as determinative of their conduct as their circumstances are.

- There is an intimate relationship between the sort of characters you create and the sort of narrative you write. In fact, they may be inseparable. You could just as easily say that the sort of characters you decide to use determines the kind of story you write as you could say that the kind of story you decide to write determines the sort of characters you use. You can't really make up your mind about one without making up your mind about the other.

- As we've said, however, these are continuums, not either/or decisions, and the same writer will try different sorts of stories and characters at different times.

- For some writers, choosing to work from the outside in or the inside out is purely instinctive: You just sit down at the keyboard and start to write in the first person or the third person. Even so, sometimes it turns out that what comes naturally doesn't work, and you may have to go back and do it a different way.

- You can also be more self-conscious and deliberate about your choices, thinking about what's more important to your story: that the characters are reflective of the larger world they inhabit or that the story is more intimate, told from inside one consciousness. How you answer that question will tell you how to create your character.

Suggested Reading

Austen, *Emma*.

Bernays and Painter, *What If?*

Brontë, *Jane Eyre*.

Hynes, *The Wild Colonial Boy*.

———, *The Lecturer's Tale*.

———, *Next*.

Writing Exercise

1. This exercise is drawn from an excellent book called *What If? Writing Exercises for Fiction Writers* by Anne Bernays and Pamela Painter: Pick a character from a story or novel that has already been written, either by you or by someone else, and make a list of everything you know or can infer about that character. Include basic features, such as the character's name, age, gender, appearance, relationship status, and so on, but also include such attributes as the character's fears, obsessions, and politics, even if they aren't explicitly mentioned in the text. Depending on the sort of narrative you're working with, you may not be able to get a complete list for any character. Such a list for Elizabeth Bennet from *Pride and Prejudice*, for example, would include a great deal about her opinions and personality but nothing about her appearance. In contrast, you can detail Sam Spade's physical appearance, but you can't find much about his opinions on anything. This exercise reinforces the idea that different sorts of stories require different types of characters.

Call Me Ishmael—Introducing a Character
Lecture 5

In our first two lectures about character, we talked in general about how characters are different from real people and from each other, but in this lecture, we'll talk about what all characters have in common—primarily, that they are all constructed out of specific details. Further, both the writer and the reader are most aware of those specific details in the moment they meet a character. In this lecture, we'll look at how you make that first impression by exploring five ways to introduce characters: (1) through straightforward description, (2) by showing the character in action, (3) through first-person narration, (4) through report by other characters, and (5) by placing the character in a specific time and place.

Straightforward Description

- Perhaps the most straightforward way to introduce a character is to simply describe him or her. For example, here are the first few lines from Joseph Conrad's *Lord Jim*:

  > He was an inch, perhaps two, under six feet, powerfully built, and he advanced straight at you with a slight stoop of the shoulders, head forward, and a fixed from-under stare which made you think of a charging bull. His voice was deep, loud, and his manner displayed a kind of dogged self-assertion which had nothing aggressive in it. … He was spotlessly neat, appareled in immaculate white from shoes to hat, and in the various Eastern ports where he got his living as a ship-chandler's water-clerk he was very popular. (p. 1)

- Here, the main character comes right off the page at the reader; we see him vividly and whole. This introduction is compelling and intriguing: Here's an attractive character who also has a bit of mystery about him. In addition, the introduction sums up the main character in a nutshell: He has something to prove to himself, and the rest of the book shows why that's so and how he goes about it.

- Conrad's introduction is also economical. Rather than lingering over details, it merely suggests physical attributes that evoke awkwardness—the slight stoop of the shoulders; the deep, loud voice—and adds a few conjectures about Jim's character—that his manner was assertive but not aggressive. Jim is shown to us here, not told; he is evoked.

- Notice that although this description is detailed and specific, it's not tied to a specific moment in Jim's life. Note, too, that this is an example of a character being introduced to us from the outside in: We're seeing how he appears to other people, not how he seems to himself.

A Character in Action

- A character who is introduced to us through a specific action comes from the book *Light* by Eva Figes:

> The sky was still dark when he opened his eyes and saw it through the uncurtained window. He was upright within seconds, out of the bed and had opened the window to study the signs. It looked good to him, the dark just beginning to fade slightly, midnight blueblack growing grey and misty, through which he could make out the last light of a dying star. It looked good to him, a calm pre-dawn hush without a breath of wind, and not a shadow of cloud in the high clear sky. He took a deep breath of air, heavy with night scents and dew on earth and foliage. His appetite for the day thoroughly aroused, his elated mood turned to energy, and he was into his dressing room, into the cold bath which set his skin tingling, humming an unknown tune under his breath. (pp. 1–2)

- This opening is dynamic in a way that the opening of *Lord Jim* is not. The character is in action, with all his senses awake, right from the first sentence. And, unlike the opening of *Lord Jim*, where we can only surmise what Jim is thinking from his appearance, Figes gives us direct access to the character's thoughts. Although we don't know it yet, this is the French artist Claude Monet, and he's just decided that this will be a good day to paint.

- Again, unlike the opening of *Lord Jim*, this opening tells us nothing of the man's physical appearance and very little about his psychology. In *Lord Jim*, it's the hint of complexity in the character that invites us to keep reading, but in this case, it's the character's energy and our curiosity to discover why he's so engaged with the natural world that propel us forward.

Direct Address to the Reader

- Another way to introduce a main character is to have him or her directly address the reader. Three of the books that are often cited as the great American novel open this way: *Moby-Dick*, *The Great Gatsby*, and *The Adventures of Huckleberry Finn*.

- A modern example of a novel whose narrator addresses the reader on the opening page is Kate Christensen's *The Epicure's Lament*:

    > October 9, 2001—All the lonely people indeed. Whoever they are, I've never been one of them. The lack of other people is a balm. It's the absence of strain and stress. I understand monks and hermits, anyone who takes a vow of silence or lives in a far-flung cave. And I thought—I hoped, rather—that I would live this way for the rest of my life, whatever time is left to me. (p. 3)

- In the subsequent paragraphs, we get some more information about this narrator, Hugo Whittier, but mainly what this opening does is draw the reader in with a specific and intriguing voice. We see immediately that the character is literate and erudite; that he not only prefers his own company, but he harbors an active hostility to other people; and that he's something of a fatalist, who doesn't expect to live much longer.

- With these types of introductions, the paragraphs that follow the opening lines start to fill in details about the character's history and current situation, but what draws us in is the fact that we're hearing individual people tell us their stories in a way that only they can. Even if we don't know what they look like or see them in action right away, we know we're hearing from a unique individual.

Introduction by Report

- Another way to introduce a character is through the eyes of other characters. Jim in *Lord Jim* is one character introduced in this way. William Faulkner also introduces Miss Emily in this way in his story "A Rose for Emily":

> When Miss Emily Grierson died, our whole town went to her funeral: the men through a sort of respectful affection for a fallen monument, the women mostly out of curiosity to see the inside of her house, which no one save an old man-servant—a combined gardener and cook—had seen in at least ten years. (*Collected Stories*, p. 119)

- Notice that the unnamed first-person narrator speaks on behalf of a town. After a few paragraphs that describe Miss Emily's history and her standoffish relationship with the town, we get a physical description of her. Interestingly, this description is also given from the point of view of the entire community; this is important in the story because Miss Emily has become an object of fascination to the townspeople.

- Faulkner deploys vivid, even pungent details to describe Miss Emily, comparing her appearance to that of a bloated corpse submerged in water. This physical description foreshadows a great deal about the character and her story without being explicit, while leaving the reader with an extremely vivid—perhaps repulsive—visual impression.

Introduction through Time or Place

- One last way of introducing a character is by the technique of situating him or her in a specific time or place. We see this approach in the opening paragraph of Robert Stone's *A Flag for Sunrise*:

> Father Egan left off writing, rose from his chair and made his way—a little unsteadily—to the bottle of Flor de Cana which he had placed across the room from his desk. The study in which he worked was lit by a Coleman lamp; he had turned the mission generators off to save kerosene. The shutters were open to receive the sea breeze and the room was cool and

pleasant. At Freddy's Chicken Shack up the road a wedding party was in progress and the revelers were singing along with the radio form Puerto Alvarado, marking the reggae beat with their own steel drums and crockery. (p. 3)

- This introduction relies almost entirely on the character's circumstances and a little bit of action rather than a description or direct access to his thoughts. We get no physical description of Father Egan, but we know from the first sentence that he's a bit of a scholar and that he's been drinking.

- The rest of the paragraph says nothing about Father Egan specifically but, with great economy and expert handling of detail, shows us that he lives at a mission near the sea in a Third World country. We get a compelling portrait of a lonely, drunken priest—cut off from any intellectual stimulation and far from home—that simultaneously uses the setting to show us the character and the character's point of view to show us the setting.

Approaches to Creating Characters
- Each of these examples is constructed with specific, evocative details, and more important, each introduction tells us at least one thing about the character that turns out to be important later on. This leads us to the question: How much does the writer have to know about a character before he or she starts writing?

- As we've said, you don't need to write a story or a novel in the same order as it will be read. You can craft the meatier parts of the character's story first, then go back and write the opening in such a way as to foreshadow what you've already written.

Character introductions rarely rely solely on one technique but often combine several: introduction by report, by physical description, and by showing the character in action.

© creativecoopmedia/iStock/Thinkstock.

- Another method is to work out all of a character's physical details, history, and context in advance. Some writers even create dossiers or journals for their major characters, crafting detailed histories and compiling idiosyncrasies before they ever put the characters in a story. This method may make it easier to decide what the characters are likely to do in various situations as the plot develops.

- Many writers follow a more indirect, exploratory, and improvisatory process. They may start with only a little bit of information about a character—perhaps even a single trait—rather than a full portrait, then gradually add details as the character develops. This method enables the writer to learn about the character in the same way that the reader will—a little at a time, through a process of discovery.

Suggested Reading

Burroway, *Writing Fiction*.

Christensen, *The Epicure's Lament*.

Conrad, *Lord Jim*.

Faulkner, "A Rose for Emily."

Figes, *Light*.

Hynes, *The Wild Colonial Boy*.

Stone, *A Flag for Sunrise*.

Writing Exercise

1. Choose someone, either in your personal life or in the public eye, about whom you know a great deal; write a paragraph about this person as if you were introducing him or her for the first time as a fictional character. Bear in mind as you write that your imaginary reader is meeting this character for the first time; thus, you should think about what sort of first impression your character makes: how he or she looks, acts, and speaks.

If you're writing about someone famous, write it as if that person isn't famous yet. If you're writing about someone you know personally, write as if that person will never read it—and don't share your results.

Characters—Round and Flat, Major and Minor
Lecture 6

As we've said, characters are constructed in different ways for different stories, and part of the reason for this is that they fulfill different functions. In some narratives, writers provide as much detail as possible about leading characters because they are the main focus of the story. In other narratives, the cast of characters is quite large, with no single dominant character. This kind of story requires the writer to sketch characters in quick, powerful strokes. Narratives also have minor characters, who often simply introduce a plot point before they disappear. These characters need to be useful and vivid and not much more. In this lecture, we'll discuss character development and the uses of different types of characters.

Flat Characters

- The distinction between round and flat characters was formulated by the English novelist E. M. Forster in his book *Aspects of the Novel*. According to Forster, flat characters are sometimes called humorous types or caricatures; their chief distinguishing feature is that they have only one chief distinguishing feature. As Forster puts it, "They are constructed round a single idea or quality."

- In *The Adventures of Huckleberry Finn*, Huck himself is round, but he is surrounded by characters of varying degrees of flatness. A good example might be Huck's father, Pap Finn, who can be summed up in a single sentence: He's a mean drunk. Pap exists mainly to further the plot: When Huck can no longer stand Pap's abuse, he fakes his own death and takes off down the Mississippi River with the slave Jim.

- The works of Charles Dickens are famously full of flat characters: the conniving and oily Uriah Heep in *David Copperfield*; the brutal criminal Bill Sikes in *Oliver Twist*; and Miss Havisham in *Great Expectations*, who was abandoned at the altar on her wedding day and has set herself apart from the rest of the world ever since.

- We might even think of such characters as the sort of people found in sitcoms: the clueless dad, the wacky neighbor, the gay best friend, the wisecracking child. Such characters are often just machines for delivering or setting up jokes, and the moment they appear on screen, we know exactly what to expect. Indeed, it's that quick identification and the sudden anticipation of something funny that often makes such characters so popular. They may be simple and predictable, but they are also reliably satisfying.

- The same is true of flat characters in fiction. "The great advantage of flat characters," says Forster, "is that they are easily recognized whenever they come in—recognized by the reader's emotional eye." This ease of recognition is important; one of the most significant traits of flat characters is that we get the whole effect of them the minute they reappear. Whenever Bill Sikes reappears in *Oliver Twist*, we immediately know that something bad will happen.

- Forster also notes a second advantage of flat characters: "that they are easily remembered by the readers afterwards." He goes on to say, "It is a convenience for an author when he can strike with his full force at once, and flat characters are very useful to him, since they never need reintroducing, never run away, have not to be watched for development, and provide their own atmosphere."

- It's important to note that a flat character must be both simple and vivid. Characters who are simple but not memorable don't really serve a purpose, and characters who are vivid but not simple are not flat characters.

- Keep in mind, too, that a flat character is not the same thing as a minor character. Even minor characters can be round. George Wilson, the working-class garage owner in *The Great Gatsby*, appears in only a few scenes, but late in the story, his grief after a tragic accident is one of the most moving scenes in the novel. Someone who was just a caricature up to that point—the clueless cuckolded husband—becomes, for a page or two, a real human being.

o   It's also true that flat characters can be important to a story. Miss Havisham is one of the most distinctive and influential characters in *Great Expectations*, yet she never develops or changes.

o   It's possible to have a story or a novel that is peopled entirely with flat characters. Sherlock Holmes is the major character in Arthur Conan Doyle's stories, but he is usually flat, producing the same effect nearly every time he appears. Holmes is also proof that flat characters are not necessarily simple or sketchy but can be quite detailed.

Round Characters

- The closest Forster comes to defining round characters is to say, "The test of a round character is whether it is capable of surprising in a convincing way. If it never surprises, it is flat. If it does not convince, it is a flat pretending to be round." The very nature of round characters is encapsulated in the metaphor we use to describe them: They curve up and away from the flat page into three dimensions. They have different sides and aspects, unlike flat characters, who appear the same from every angle.

- Round characters are also richer, deeper, more mysterious, and more unpredictable than flat characters. They can do all the things a flat character can do—come vividly to life, be memorable and instantly recognizable, and be engaging and entertaining—but they can also surprise, delight, and disappoint us in the same way as real people. Further, as Forster notes, they don't just surprise us, but they surprise us in a convincing way.
  o   Flat characters can be surprising, but they provide the sort of mechanical surprise we find in a mystery or a spy novel, where a trustworthy character suddenly turns out to be the murderer or the double agent. Although this kind of a surprise can be effective, it also sometimes comes across as a kind of cheating, and our response can sometimes be a groan or a roll of the eyes.

o   In contrast, the kind of surprise we get from a round character should evoke both shock and the strong feeling of inevitability. The reader thinks, "Of course! I should have seen that coming." When a round character surprises us, we're delighted or moved in ways that flat characters can't manage—by sudden acts of kindness or cruelty that we didn't expect but that we believe the moment we see them. Round characters can also break our hearts in ways that flat characters can't, by disappointing us in a lifelike way.

o   Round characters should be both surprising and inevitable so that whatever happens to them is probably the only way things could have turned out—not because of circumstance necessarily, but because of their own complex, flawed natures drove them to it.

- As mentioned in an earlier lecture, fictional people are different from real people because we can know what they're thinking, which is perhaps another definition of roundness. This is the case even if the writer never actually shows us what the character is thinking, as long as the potential for the writer to show us is present. By the same token, characters may be round as long as they have the potential to change, even if they never actually do. Some of the most heartbreaking people in fiction are rounded characters who, for whatever reason, lose their nerve or are defeated by circumstance.

- The complexity or roundness of a character isn't necessarily defined entirely by psychology but can be defined by circumstances, as well. Mrs. Dalloway is round because we are inside her mind at every moment, listening to her private thoughts. In a series of detective novels by Denise Mina, we see inside the mind of the main character, Paddy Meehan, but much of the richness of that character comes from her circumstances—from Mina's skillful evocation of the dank, melancholy world of working-class Glasgow in the 1970s and 1980s.

Characters and Conflict

- Perhaps the most important distinction between flat and round characters has to do with the idea of conflict in fiction. A useful generalization here is that all characters want something or are driven by something; all characters have something at stake in the narrative.

- Flat characters want only one simple thing: Sherlock Holmes wants to solve a mystery; Miss Havisham wants revenge against men. Round characters, in contrast, want something complicated, ineffable, or ambiguous. They may be conflicted about what they want, often to the point that they have no clear idea what they're actually looking for.

- With Anna Karenina, for example, not only is it hard for the reader to pin down what's driving her, but Anna herself can't articulate exactly what's lacking in her life. She wants her lover, Count Vronsky, yet having him doesn't satisfy her. Her desperation grows as the costs of leaving her husband and losing her child mount up. There's something unreachable in Anna that makes her frustrating, poignant, and supremely human.

© Szepy/iStock/Thinkstock.

By including a bit of description for flat characters—"a sour waiter brought her a cup of coffee"—you hint at the possibility of a richer, fuller world in your work.

Character Development

- Distinctions between major and minor characters offer us a number of insights into character development. First of all, minor characters receive less space and attention in a narrative than major characters do. You don't need a complicated backstory for a waiter to bring your main character a cup of coffee, although you may want to add a hint of description to give that waiter a bit of substance.

- As for the distinction between round and flat, you may not notice which a character is until after you've created him or her, but at some point, you should think deliberately about the function of each character, major or minor, flat or round, in your narrative.
    - Whether you construct characters in advance or let them develop organically as you write the narrative, at some point, you will come to a visceral understanding of how your characters figure in the story and how simple or complex their desires are.

    - You may discover that a character you originally conceived of as round and complex actually functions only to move the plot along. In that case, you have a flat character, and you can draft or revise your story to ensure that he or she is memorable but without constructing a detailed backstory.

    - You may also discover that a character you meant to be minor turns out to be rounder and more important than you originally thought. If that's the case, you can make the introduction of that character a little fuller so that his or her reappearance in the story seems believable.

Suggested Reading

Dickens, *Great Expectations*.

Fitzgerald, *The Great Gatsby*.

Forster, *Aspects of the Novel*.

Mina, *Field of Blood*.

Twain, *The Adventures of Huckleberry Finn*.

1. Using a story you like or a completed draft of one of your own stories, list all the characters and describe what each character wants as briefly as possible. Using only what the story itself says about the character, you should be able to determine quickly who is flat versus round and who is major versus minor. Sherlock Holmes's entry might say, "He wants to solve the crime and impress everyone with his brilliance." Anna Karenina's entry might say, "She wants the sort of passion from another man that she's never had from her husband, but in truth, she doesn't really know what she wants." If you find yourself pausing over one of your own characters and wondering what he or she wants to do, you may discover that you have some additional work to do in character development.

The Mechanics of Writing Dialogue
Lecture 7

As we saw in an earlier lecture, fictional people are often more memorable than real people because they are less complicated and more vivid. By the same token, dialogue in fiction can be more vivid and memorable than real speech because it is more focused and coherent than real speech. Further, in fiction, dialogue has a purpose—usually to evoke character, advance the plot, or provide exposition—while real-life dialogue is often rambling, incoherent, or dull. In this first lecture on dialogue, we'll talk about the mechanics of writing dialogue and some basic techniques for using dialogue tags and for mixing speech, action, and exposition.

Rules of Dialogue

- The mechanical rules of dialogue, including frequent paragraph breaks and the use of quotation marks, serve two fundamental purposes: to separate direct quotations by the characters from the rest of the narrative and to clarify for the reader just who is speaking at any given time. Some excellent writers have ignored these conventions in writing dialogue, but in most cases, using nonstandard formats or punctuation for dialogue is not worth the extra effort it requires from the reader to interpret the text.

- The first rule for writing dialogue is that all direct quotations should be set apart from the rest of the text by quotation marks, and the second rule is that every time a new character speaks or the speaker changes, that first line of dialogue should be set apart with a paragraph break. Also, the beginning of a direct quotation should always begin with a capital letter.

- In its most basic form, a *dialogue tag* is simply the name of a character or a pronoun standing in for the name, plus some variation of the verb *say*: "He said," "Bob exclaimed," and so on. The rules for punctuating dialogue tags can be a little tricky.

o   Because the dialogue tag is not part of the actual quotation, it should never be included within the quotation marks.

o   Sometimes a dialogue tag comes in the middle of the quoted sentence; when that happens, the first half of the quotation is set off by a comma and a quotation mark, the dialogue tag is followed with a comma, and the second half of the sentence begins with a quotation mark and a lowercase letter.

o   If a dialogue tag appears between two complete sentences, then the dialogue tag ends with a period, and the second sentence starts with a capital letter.

Reasons for Dialogue Tags
- In general, dialogue tags are necessary for three reasons: (1) to introduce a character who is speaking for the first time, (2) to identify the speakers when two or more people are speaking, or (3) to get across necessary information or a bit context that isn't clear from the dialogue itself, such as exactly how someone is saying something. Let's look at these three reasons in turn.

- A dialogue tag is used when you're introducing a character for the first time or returning to a character at the beginning of a new chapter or scene. However, a dialogue tag may be unnecessary in some situations, such as a scene with a single character who is calling for help. A dialogue tag may also be deferred for dramatic effect, although there's usually the expectation that the speaker will be identified fairly quickly.

- The second reason for using dialogue tags is to identify speakers when two or more people are talking. The usual practice here is to identify each speaker with his or her first line of dialogue, though again, there can be exceptions. If you have more than two speakers in a scene, you will have to use more dialogue tags to keep them straight for the reader.

- The third use of dialogue tags requires more judgment and skill than the first two but is just as essential: using tags to provide some context or nuance that isn't conveyed by the dialogue itself or to clear up an ambiguity.

- o Consider this simple example: "'I love you,' she said." In most cases, the context for this statement is likely to be clear from the narrative, but it is easy to imagine situations in which that statement could be spoken in multiple ways by a character or understood in multiple ways by the reader.

- o If you don't want the declaration to be ambiguous, you can clarify it by adding a more descriptive verb or an adverb: "'I love you,' she sobbed"; "'I love you,' she said casually." Instead of altering the dialogue tag, you might also italicize one or more of the words in the dialogue to show the speaker's emphasis: "'*I* love you,' she said"; "'I *love* you,' she said."

If you have a conversation between two characters that goes on for less than a page, you can probably get away with identifying the speakers at the beginning, then not mentioning them again.

Using Dialogue Tags

- Another rule of thumb for dialogue tags is to use them sparingly and keep them as simple as possible. The more you can rely on the speech of the characters to convey the emotion and reveal who's saying what, the better. In fact, in general, you should use dialogue tags only when it would otherwise be impossible to tell who is speaking or when the context needs clarification.

- Keep in mind, however, that you shouldn't be too sparing with dialogue tags. On the one hand, you don't want to be obtrusive or redundant, but on the other hand, you don't want the reader to get confused. You want to strike a balance between letting the characters' actual words carry the weight of the conversation and risking that the reader will lose track of who's saying what.

- Even if only two people are talking, a dialogue tag may be necessary later in the conversation, especially if it goes on for a long time and isn't broken up with much action or exposition.
  - Crime stories, for example, often feature long conversations in which an investigator asks a suspect or witness a long series of questions. Some writers introduce the two characters at the start, then dispense with dialogue tags entirely, assuming that it's clear from the dialogue who's asking questions and who's answering them.

  - However, even if the writer is careful to distinguish between the two speakers at the start of a long exchange, at times, readers can get confused about who's speaking. In these cases, it's helpful for the writer to include a dialogue tag every few lines as a signpost for readers.

- Again, when you use dialogue tags, keep them as simple as possible, avoiding excessive description or explanation. It may be helpful to use a stronger verb or an adverb in some instances, but in general, the dialogue itself should carry as much of the meaning as possible, without unnecessary help. "'You're a clumsy idiot,' said the coach" is probably clear enough without any extra emphasis; "'You're a clumsy idiot,' said the coach disparagingly" is unnecessary, given that the coach is obviously disparaging his listener.

Interweaving Dialogue Tags with Narrative
- The most graceful way to write dialogue is not to separate it from the rest of the narrative but to interweave the two. In real life, people don't always stop what they're doing to talk to each other but carry on conversations while doing other things. Further, each participant in real-

life conversations takes note of the other person's facial expressions, gestures, and body language. Dialogue usually works best when it is an integral part of a scene that combines the thoughts, actions, and speech of the characters.

- Consider a dialogue passage from the novel *Next*, in which the main character, Kevin, an academic editor, is meeting with Eileen, the professor who has just become his new boss. In the following bare bones version of this passage, with just the speech and no action or description, it's obvious that Eileen is being imperious and condescending, while Kevin is nervous and defensive.

"I've seen you at the gym," Eileen said.

"Yes," Kevin said.

"I assume that's your lunch hour?"

"Yeah, I play a pickup game with some guys two, three days a week."

"So the game itself lasts, what, forty-five minutes?"

"Maybe a little less."

"So by the time you walk over there, change your clothes, warm up, play the game, shower and walk back to your office, that's what? An hour and a quarter? An hour and a half?"

"Come on, Eileen, I see you at the gym all the time."

"I'm not on the clock. May I call you Kevin?"

"Of course."

"Kevin, you're not salaried like I'm salaried. Do we understand each other?"

"Perfectly."

"I'll look over your budget, and we'll have a talk about it, soon," said Eileen.

- In a more fleshed-out version of the same passage, the dialogue is integrated with the setting, the physical presence of the two characters, and Kevin's thoughts as Eileen dresses him down. Again, the exchange begins as follows:

   "I've seen you at the gym," she said, still standing.

   "Yes." Kevin brightened—she remembers me!

- With just a bit more description of the action and a glimpse into Kevin's thoughts, even these two lines give us subtle cues that the conversation won't end well: The fact that Eileen remains standing should be a warning sign for Kevin, but he misreads her mood and "brightens," thinking that she remembers him from the gym. He obviously didn't expect her to remember him but thinks the fact that they both use the gym might serve as common ground between them.

- As the second version progresses, we learn, through some simple details, that Eileen can be cold, at least with a subordinate: She speaks with "icy politesse," and she looks at Kevin with "glacially blue eyes." We also infer that she has little respect for Kevin from the fact that she continues to sort through the carpet swatches for her new office while she talks to him. Indeed, her gestures act as a counterpoint to the dialogue, showing her physically judging something as she verbally judges Kevin.

- We learn more about Kevin in the second version. Because the novel is told from his point of view, we have access to Kevin's thoughts, and as the dialogue progresses, we don't have to infer his growing anxiety about his meeting with his new boss, but we can see it happening in real time. The dialogue and Kevin's internal monologue reinforce each other.

- In the first version, with the dialogue alone, we are witnessing a conversation, but in the second version, we are participating in it, at least from Kevin's point of view. We feel that he starts to feel smaller under Eileen's icy gaze, and we feel him vibrating with repressed rage as he leaves the office. That effect is the result of interweaving the dialogue with visual cues, physical sensations, and access to at least one character's thoughts.

Suggested Reading

Faulkner, *The Sound and the Fury*.

Hynes, *Next*.

McCarthy, *Blood Meridian*.

———, *The Road*.

Writing Exercise

1. Write out a dialogue, perhaps half a page or a page, between two people who are at cross purposes to each other: one is in love and the other isn't, for example, or one wants something that the other doesn't want to give up. In the first version, write the dialogue like a play, with no dialogue tags or even the names of the characters—just the dialogue itself. Then, add layers to that initial dialogue. Try a version with basic dialogue tags, then a version with slightly more descriptive dialogue tags, then a version with some action and physical description, then a version with access to the characters' thoughts, and so on. Each version will likely have a very different effect. Depending on what effect you prefer, choose the version that you think is best.

Integrating Dialogue into a Narrative
Lecture 8

In our first lecture about dialogue, we said that speech in fiction, no matter how rambling, digressive, elaborate, or colorful, must serve a purpose, and that, generally speaking, we can categorize those purposes as evoking character, telling the story, and providing exposition. In this lecture, we'll talk in more detail about how dialogue can serve those purposes and about finding the balance between dialogue and other parts of the narrative. Some stories and novels are made up almost entirely of dialogue, while some stories use it only as a seasoning. Deciding just how much, how often, and how effectively your characters speak will also help you decide just what sort of story you're writing.

Dialogue to Evoke Character

- Character is evoked by a variety of techniques used together or in close succession, including description, action, dialogue, interior monologue, and so on. Although dialogue doesn't always bear the brunt of characterization, it's not unusual for individual characters to speak in distinctive ways. Dickens, for example, is known for his colorful secondary characters, who often use catchphrases or speak in a particular dialect. George R. R. Martin, who has proven to be a sort of a latter-day Dickens, also uses this technique with the characters in his fantasy series *A Song of Ice and Fire*.

- It's perhaps more common for a character to have a distinctive pattern of speech than an oft-repeated catchphrase. The perpetually debt-ridden Mr. Micawber in Dickens's *David Copperfield*, for example, is distinguished by his comically elaborate way of expressing himself. This technique works well in narratives where the characters are a bit more extreme than they might be in a more realistic narrative.

- In the 19th century, many writers used dialect, with the result that much 19th-century fiction is now unreadable. In *Dracula*, for example, there's a long, almost incomprehensible passage in which Bram Stoker tries to reproduce the accent of an old sailor from Yorkshire. The use of dialect, as in Mark Twain's *Huckleberry Finn* or Zora Neale Hurston's *Their Eyes Were Watching God*, can also come across as offensive or stereotypical.

- o The problem with dialect, then, is twofold: It's often difficult to follow, and unless the entire work is written in dialect (as *Huckleberry Finn* is, for example), dialect can set certain speakers apart as "not normal," with the result that it's difficult for readers to think of them as fully human.

- o Today, most writers evoke dialect in a more subtle fashion, relying on word choice and variations in grammar and syntax to suggest regional speech or social class, rather than trying to reproduce it in every detail. Consider Toni Morrison's *Beloved*, a novel about an African American family in the aftermath of the Civil War. The characters speak a straightforward, conversational, modern English, with just an occasional hint of slang or nonstandard syntax or grammar to suggest their race, social class, and era.

- • As mentioned earlier, people in fiction generally have something at stake or something they want, and the best way to evoke character with dialogue is to have them express what they want, though not necessarily directly. In other words, creating effective dialogue for a character involves inhabiting that character's point of view, not necessarily reproducing an accent or a particular pattern of speech.

Creating a character's speech is less about reproducing a real-life dialect and more about who that character is and how his or her speech might reflect the immediate situation; a nervous character, for example, may stammer or ramble.

- • It's also true that characters sometimes just talk—not about what they want or about the situation they're in—but about something tangential or even completely unrelated, and the sound of their voices serves to evoke the speaker and the milieu.

Dialogue to Tell the Story

- George V. Higgins's *The Friends of Eddie Coyle* tells the story of an armed robbery and its aftermath mainly through a series of monologues and conversations, some of which read almost like a play by Samuel Beckett. Many crime narratives or detective stories are told almost entirely through dialogue; the modern master of this was Elmore Leonard, the author of *Get Shorty* and many other books.

- Mystery narratives often consist of two stories told in tandem, namely, the story of the investigation, which is usually chronological, and the story of the events leading up to the crime, which the reader usually gets in bits and pieces from dialogue as the detective listens to statements from witnesses or suspects. Many, if not most, of the Sherlock Holmes stories are structured this way, as is *The Maltese Falcon*, which consists almost entirely of scenes in which characters argue, plead, and negotiate with each other.

- However, it isn't just crime fiction that uses dialogue to move the plot along. Another dialogue-filled novel is Jane Austen's *Pride and Prejudice*, in which many of the most important encounters and incidents take place in conversation. In one scene at a ball, the novel's heroine, Elizabeth Bennet, finds herself dancing against her will with Mr. Darcy, the novel's haughty leading man, and the two verbally spar with each other for three pages.

- It's important to note that not every conversation in fiction is a competition or argument. As we've said, people in fiction speak to each other for all the reasons people in real life do, and people in fiction are just as capable of misdirection, confusion, and reticence as real people are. Some of the greatest scenes in literature feature characters who are not actually talking about what's at stake in the scene but about something else entirely. Dialogue can hide a character's intent as well as show it, and often, the meaning of a dialogue is more present in what the characters don't say rather than in what they do.

- A wonderful example is from part 6 of Tolstoy's *Anna Karenina*, at the start of chapter 5, in which two minor characters, a middle-aged man named Sergei Ivanovich and a middle-aged woman named Varenka, are picking mushrooms in the forest. Each is in love with the other, and not only is Sergei working up his nerve to ask for Varenka's hand, but Varenka is expecting him to propose at any moment.

- At the crucial moment, Sergei loses his nerve. Instead of proposing to Varenka, he asks her the difference between two types of mushrooms. With that question and Varenka's response, both characters realize that the marriage will never take place. Perhaps the most heartbreaking feature of the scene is the fact that the dialogue has nothing to do with what's really on the characters' minds. They're thinking about love, but they're talking about mushrooms.

- Even though the dialogue itself does not actually address the matter at hand or directly express any of the repressed emotion, it's crucial to the devastating effect of the scene. In fact, the scene would not work without it. What makes the scene work is that the intensity of the characters' private emotions is immediately juxtaposed on the page with their banal statements about mushrooms.

- Such oblique use of dialogue has become even more subtle in contemporary short fiction. An expert practitioner of this technique is the Nobel Prize–winning Canadian writer Alice Munro. Her story "Walker Brothers Cowboy" is about a married salesman named Ben who takes his two children with him one day into rural Ontario, where he stops at the house of a woman named Nora whom he hasn't seen in years.
    - The story is narrated in the present tense by the man's daughter, but the voice is clearly that of an adult looking back on a situation she didn't understand when it took place. Near the end of the story, Nora plays a phonograph record and makes the narrator, Ben's unnamed daughter, dance with her. Nora then stands in front of Ben and asks him to dance.

o   Munro's narrator never directly says, "This woman was an old flame of my father's, and now she wants him back," but instead, Munro allows us to experience the situation as the narrator did, picking up the cues from what she hears and observes: the way Nora begs Ben to dance with her and the way he refuses, the way Nora's arms hang "loose and hopeful" and her face shines with delight.

o   Unlike the more direct and instrumental dialogue in *The Maltese Falcon* or *Pride and Prejudice*, where characters speak directly to the matter at hand, and unlike the scene in *Anna Karenina*, where Tolstoy makes the subtext explicit by telling us what the characters are thinking, Munro's dialogue is oblique, carrying a great deal of emotion but stopping just short of addressing its root cause.

Dialogue to Provide Exposition

*   The most mechanical use to which dialogue can be put is to provide exposition, that is, to have one character explain the backstory or impart some necessary information, ostensibly to another character but, in reality, to the reader. When it's done stylishly and evokes character at the same time, this technique can be quite entertaining.

*   One expert practitioner of expository dialogue is the novelist Elmore Leonard. His novel *Cuba Libre* is about an American who gets caught up in the Spanish-American War in 1898. In the first chapter of the novel, two of the major characters, a couple of cowboys who are planning to ship some horses to Cuba, talk about the deal. In the course of the dialogue, they fill in their own backstories and provide a quick-and-dirty history of the war in Cuba.

*   Leonard's approach in the scene is relatively painless, but it's not as seamless or engrossing as the rest of the book. In fact, we've all read books or seen movies in which an especially flat minor character appears to explain the backstory, then disappears, never to be heard

from again. The sole function of Dr. Mortimer in Conan Doyle's *The Hound of the Baskervilles*, for example, is to appear from time to time and explain things.

- There are three alternative methods to trying to shoehorn exposition into dialogue.
    - The simplest of these is to violate the "show, don't tell" rule and provide the information directly to the reader in the narration itself. Some authors write a dramatic opening chapter or two to draw the reader in, then put the main narrative on hold to fill in the background on the main character.

    - If your story is told in the first person and the narrator is privy to the information you need to get across, you can have him or her fill in the background directly.

    - If the information must come from a particular character at a particular moment in the story, you might use *indirect dialogue*, which is a summary of what a character has said, without using his or her exact words.

Suggested Reading

Austen, *Pride and Prejudice*.

Dickens, *David Copperfield*.

Hammett, *The Maltese Falcon*.

Higgins, *The Friends of Eddie Coyle*.

Leonard, *Cuba Libre*.

Morrison, *Beloved*.

Munro, "Walker Brothers Cowboy."

Tolstoy, *Anna Karenina*.

1. Without invading the participants' privacy, take a fragment of real-life conversation—one you may have been party to or a brief exchange you may have overheard—and try to construct a more lengthy and detailed dialogue out of it. The conversation could be something as banal as one person asking, "Is this seat taken?" and the other replying, "No, it isn't," or it could be freighted with significance, such as one woman saying to another, "So what did you tell him?" and the other woman saying, "I told him no." Whatever fragment you use, start by figuring out what the next line would be, then try to spin as much out of it as you can, incorporating a variety of the uses to which dialogue can be put. In other words, starting with just two overheard lines, use dialogue to create a couple of characters and tell a story.

And Then—Turning a Story into a Plot
Lecture 9

A s noted earlier in the course, literature is the creation of order out of chaos—the creation of meaning and structure out of reality, which is otherwise meaningless and without structure. We've already seen several ways in which fiction imposes order on chaos: When we evoke a person, a scene, or a situation, we select the details that best get across what we want the reader to see and understand. When we write dialogue, we suggest real speech without actually reproducing it, thus imposing purpose on speech. But perhaps the most obvious way that fiction imposes order on chaos is through the creation of stories and plots, which will be the subject of this and the next five lectures.

Introduction to Plot

- Given the prevalence of stories in all human cultures and in our own personal lives, it's easy to think that stories occur naturally in the world, like fruit hanging from a tree, and that all a writer has to do is pluck them. But the reality is more complicated than that.

- If literature is the creation of order out of chaos, it follows that all fiction has a structure. Even for narrative works that don't have plots, all fiction can be broken down into a few fundamental components: a situation or context, at least one character, a conflict of some sort, and a resolution to that conflict. All these elements are inextricably linked in every work of fiction, and if you're missing one of them, your narrative won't work.

- The initial situation needs to be dramatically productive, that is, it needs to be a situation that will produce a conflict, and the character or characters need to have some sort of relationship to that situation. The conflict can be external to the character, or it can be an internal conflict within the character, and the resolution must resolve that conflict in some believable and dramatically satisfying way, though not necessarily happily or pleasantly.

- All fiction must also possess a quality that the writer and teacher John Gardner called "profluence," which he defined as the feeling you have when you're reading a novel or short story that you're getting someplace. Another way to think of this quality is as forward momentum.

  o Whether it's a highly plotted, complicated story, such as *Game of Thrones*, or a modernist, plotless masterpiece, such as *Mrs. Dalloway*, a book or story needs to give the reader a reason to keep turning pages.

  o Profluence doesn't necessarily mean that a story has a plot per se; there are other reasons besides plot to keep reading. Sometimes, you read to gain a deeper understanding of the central character, as is the case in Anton Chekhov's plotless story "The Kiss." Or you might read simply to inhabit a strange and richly detailed world or to enjoy an author's writing style.

Defining *Plot*

- Although our culture is dominated by the traditional narrative structure, some writers remain uneasy with the idea of plot. John Gardner, in his book *The Art of Fiction*, called plotting "the hardest job a writer has." E. M. Forster wrote that a story "can only have one merit: that of making the audience want to know what happens next. And conversely, it can only have one fault: that of making the audience not want to know what happens next." As we'll see, however, creating an engrossing plot is one of the most satisfying things a writer can do and no more arbitrary an act than creating characters.

- Think back to the story we concocted in our first lecture about Sarah and Brad, the couple at the baseball game whose marriage was on the rocks. We could take that same situation and tell it from any number of different points of view—Sarah's, Brad's, a mutual friend's, even from a godlike, omniscient point of view. We could also play with the order of events, telling the story in a strictly chronological fashion or starting from the moment when Sarah tells Brad she's unhappy, then showing their previous relationship in flashbacks.

- Done well, each version of Sarah and Brad's story could be satisfying and meaningful, yet each would be completely different from all the others. Plotting is an incredibly powerful tool, but like any powerful tool, it's difficult to handle. If you don't take enough control over it, your plot will seem loose and formless, with no forward momentum—a series of events that has no particular importance or obvious meaning. But if you use narrative too forcefully, you could end up with something melodramatic, mechanical, contrived, and unbelievable.

- How do we create stories out of formless events and create an order that seems both satisfying and lifelike? Let's return to Forster again, who clarified this problem by making a distinction between stories and plots. In a famous passage in *Aspects of the Novel*, he defines a story as simply a series of events linked by their chronology, but he defines a plot as a series of events linked by cause and effect.

The Story-Plot Continuum

- We might think of the same distinction between stories and plots as opposite ends of a continuum, with the most basic, chronological story at one end of the continuum and the most subtle plot at the other.

The fact that children insist on hearing the same story told in exactly the same way reinforces the idea that with a good story, it's not just how it turns out that counts but how you get there.

- The simplest and often the most addictive stories are the ones that simply answer the question "And then?" These are the stories we like best as children, the ones that we beg our parents to finish for us because we can't stand not knowing how they turn out. As we get older, the desire to learn the answer to "And then?" never really leaves us. Much of the pleasure we derive from even a mediocre Hollywood blockbuster comes from watching the story unfold one plot point at a time—even if the story is predictable.

- Closer to the middle of the continuum between story and plot are such blockbuster series as the Harry Potter books by J. K. Rowling or the epic fantasy series *A Song of Ice and Fire* by George R. R. Martin, better known in its HBO version as *Game of Thrones*. The overarching story of each of these series of novels moves relentlessly forward chronologically, yet each is more complicated than a simple chronology.

  o Much of the narrative momentum of Harry Potter involves Harry figuring out what happened between his parents and the villain Voldemort before he was born. We get this information in flashbacks, stories from other characters, mysterious documents, and magic visions, all of which Rowling uses to mix up the chronology of the backstory. Each of these nonchronological additions moves the Harry Potter books away from Forster's simple chronological "tapeworm"—what will happen to Harry next?—and toward his idea of a plot— why is Harry so important?

  o The construction of *A Song of Ice and Fire* is even more complicated. The fictional world of Westeros has a long, convoluted history that precedes the events of the first book, and the story is told from the point of view of many characters, sometimes returning to earlier events told from a different point of view. The books have tremendous forward momentum, but still, much of the pleasure in reading them comes from elements other than the plot. We want to know the answer to "And then?" but there is much to savor that doesn't relate to that question.

The Literary End of the Continuum

- At the literary end of the story-plot continuum is Joseph Conrad's novel *Lord Jim*. This book has one of the most complex plots in modern literature, yet the basic events of the story are fairly simple.

  o Jim, a romantic young Englishman, seeks his fortune as a sailor in the seas of South and Southeast Asia in the late 19th century. Even before his career at sea has properly gotten started, he becomes the first mate of a rusting old freighter carrying Muslim pilgrims across the Indian Ocean to Mecca. When the freighter, called the *Patna*, collides with some unseen object in the water and threatens to sink, the rest of the crew prepares to abandon ship, leaving the pilgrims to die. At the last minute, Jim betrays his own sense of honor by jumping into the lifeboat along with the other crew members.

- After Jim and the rest of the crew are rescued and arrive in port, they learn that the *Patna* didn't sink. The rest of the crew disappears, but Jim turns himself in to accept responsibility for what happened. At a tribunal of sea captains, he is stripped of his seaman's license, and his career and reputation are ruined.

- After the trial, Jim drifts from job to job across Southeast Asia until he decides to accept a dangerous job far upriver on a remote island, where he helps a village defeat an oppressive warlord and win its freedom. By the end of the story, it looks as though Jim has found peace and redemption at last when, in a final series of incidents, his past returns to destroy him.

- Told chronologically, *Lord Jim* sounds like an action-packed adventure story, but the complexity of its plotting makes it into something richer and more melancholy. In telling the story, Conrad not only jumbles the chronology, but he also tells the story through several layers of point of view.

- If *Lord Jim* is told chronologically, it's a simple tale about a young man who makes a bad mistake and tries to redeem himself. But told by Conrad, through various narrators, with the story starting in the middle and looping backward and forward, *Lord Jim* becomes an intimate and intense psychological study of a character who is destroyed by his idealistic conception of honor rather than redeemed by it.

- Despite the complexity of Conrad's plot, *Lord Jim* may be the most realistic of all the narratives discussed in this lecture. Chronological narratives seem lifelike because we experience our own lives in chronological order. Conrad's method doesn't mimic the way Jim's life happens, but it does mimic, in a very lifelike way, the manner in which most of us learn about other people in our lives. The result is a much more intense and intimate experience of the character because it forces readers to assemble the chronology of Jim's life, leading to greater understanding and compassion.

- It isn't true that simple storytelling is inferior, and complex, nonchronological, modernist plotting is superior. But it is true that the two approaches reach different regions of a reader's heart and brain and serve different functions for the writer.

Suggested Reading

Conrad, *Lord Jim*.

Eliot, *Middlemarch*.

Forster, *Aspects of the Novel*.

Gardner, *The Art of Fiction*.

Martin, *A Song of Ice and Fire*.

Rowling, *Harry Potter and the Sorcerer's Stone*.

Writing Exercise

1. List all the major plot points of a story you admire or a story of your own, but write them out on index cards, one plot point to a card, in the order they actually appear in the story. If the story is a narrative that is told out of chronological order, try putting the cards in chronological order and see how that sequence changes the effect of the narrative. If the story is a narrative that already moves chronologically, lay the cards out and see what happens if you start rearranging them. If you want to be especially bold, shuffle the cards and try retelling the story in whatever order they end up in. Deciding how to arrange or shuffle the events of a narrative is a large part of deciding what you want the reader to take away from it.

Plotting with the Freytag Pyramid
Lecture 10

The basic structure of a traditional plot—situation, conflict, resolution—was first codified by Aristotle in the *Poetics*, in which he defines the elements that make up a tragic drama. Aristotle was the first to state that a story should have a beginning, a middle, and an end; that the events of the plot should be causally connected and self-contained; and that the ending of the plot—particularly the plot of a tragedy—should provide both closure and catharsis. More commonly referenced today than Aristotle is Freytag's pyramid, a diagram of dramatic structure based on Aristotle's theory. In this lecture, we'll look at the pyramid, using the film version of *The Wizard of Oz* as an example.

The Wizard of Oz and Freytag's Pyramid

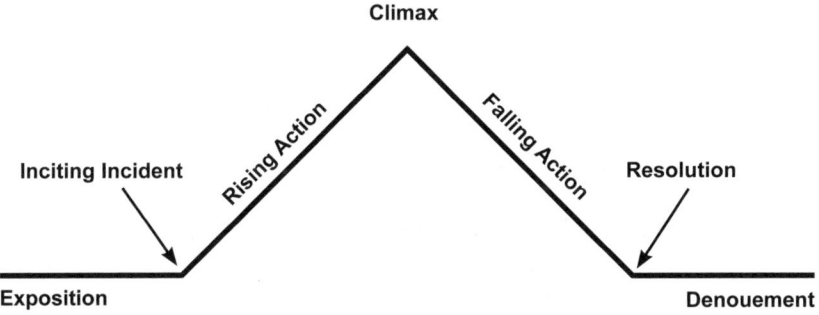

- According to Freytag's pyramid, the exposition stage of a story sets the scene and introduces the characters. In *The Wizard of Oz*, the exposition is everything that happens from the beginning of the film to the tornado: We meet all the major characters; Dorothy runs away with Toto and meets Professor Marvel; and on her way back to the farm, Dorothy is overtaken by the storm.

- Next comes the inciting action, which is the event that introduces conflict into the story. This bit is tricky with *The Wizard of Oz* because there are two elements in the story that might be called the conflict.

  o One is the conflict between Dorothy and Miss Gulch because Miss Gulch wants Dorothy's dog put to sleep. This is what causes Dorothy to run away from home, leading to the blow to the head she receives during the tornado. In that sense, we might consider Miss Gulch's threat the inciting moment.

  o But this conflict becomes more complicated when the tornado transports Dorothy to the Land of Oz. There, Dorothy's house lands on the Wicked Witch of the East and kills her, and the Wicked Witch of the West threatens to kill Dorothy in revenge. However, this is actually the same as the first conflict because the Wicked Witch of the West is Miss Gulch in her Oz incarnation, and in both incarnations, she wants to harm Dorothy.

  o There's also another potential conflict that arises after Dorothy lands in Oz: the fact that she wants to go home, but nobody knows how to send her back to Kansas. The two conflicts— Dorothy versus the Wicked Witch and Dorothy's quest to go home—are linked and become even more explicitly linked later on.

- The rising action is the part where the plot becomes more complicated and exciting, building tension. In *The Wizard of Oz*, the rising action includes Dorothy's departure from Munchkinland; her meetings with the Scarecrow, the Tin Man, and the Cowardly Lion; her arrival in Emerald City; her first audience with the wizard; and her capture by the witch.

  o During this party of the story, small obstacles are thrown in the path of Dorothy and her companions, and the two conflicts mentioned earlier are reemphasized. Once Dorothy and her companions arrive in Oz, the witch spells out "Surrender Dorothy" in the sky, and Dorothy, trembling before the flaming head of the wizard, asks for his help in returning home. The two conflicts are then explicitly linked when the wizard tells Dorothy that he'll help her get back to Kansas if she brings him the witch's broomstick.

- o Dorothy and her companions then face their most difficult challenge, with Dorothy getting carried away by the flying monkeys and her companions breaking into the witch's castle to rescue her.

- The climax is the most dramatic and exciting event in a story. In *The Wizard of Oz*, the climax comes when Dorothy and her friends are trapped in the witch's castle, and Dorothy kills the witch by dousing her with a bucket of water. At that moment, much of the film's tension is released because at least one of the conflicts, the one between Dorothy and the witch, is ended, and the plot begins its descent down the other side of the pyramid.

- The next element is the falling action, which is made up of the events that result directly from the moment of climax. The element after that is called the resolution, where the character's conflict is resolved.
  - o After Dorothy has killed the witch, she takes the broomstick back to the wizard. He solves the problems of the Scarecrow, the Tin Man, and the Cowardly Lion and agrees to take Dorothy back to Kansas himself. This is the falling action: It shows the results of the death of the witch, but it doesn't resolve Dorothy's second conflict, the fact that she wants to go home to Kansas.

  - o The resolution comes when the wizard accidentally takes off in his balloon without Dorothy, and Dorothy learns from Glinda the Good Witch that she could have taken herself back to Kansas at any time by using the ruby slippers. At this point, Dorothy's conflict is finally resolved—the threat from the witch is liquidated, and she realizes that she always had the power to go home.

- The denouement is the ending of the story, when order is restored. At this stage, we are often shown the characters one more time so that we can see what happened to them. In *The Wizard of Oz*, it's the final scene in Dorothy's bedroom, where she is reunited with Aunt Em and Uncle Henry and the now-familiar farmhands.
  - In some stories, the denouement simply shows that order has been restored, and the world is now back the way it was. But this isn't usually the case, and it's certainly not the case in *The Wizard of Oz*.

  - Dorothy is back home, but everything is not back to the way it was before she went to Oz. Dorothy's understanding of herself and her place in the world have profoundly changed.

Pros and Cons of Traditional Structure
- The structure outlined by Freytag's pyramid is sturdy, reliable, and ubiquitous, but it can, at times, seem like a straightjacket. With many conventionally plotted novels, we can guess the ending after the first few pages or even from the jacket copy. Sometimes we feel both reassured and annoyed at the same story: You may guess during the first 10 pages that the sparring lovers will eventually get together, but you might be irritated if, at the end, they don't really like each other and wind up with other people. The predictable can be both seductive and disappointing at the same time.

- Even so, this particular narrative structure has proved to be surprisingly adaptable, especially considering that it was originally conceived to apply to stage tragedies. The plays Aristotle was familiar with usually focused on the fate of a single central character, such as Oedipus or Medea, not novels that incorporate numerous characters. Yet this structure can be applied to everything from comedy to tragedy, thrillers to love stories, and *Hamlet* to *Star Wars*.

- For writers who are just starting out, this narrative structure can be a useful set of training wheels, especially if you're uneasy about plotting. It's so common in our culture, in fact, than many writers adopt it instinctively, without even thinking about it.

Complicating Traditional Plots

- Perhaps the Freytag pyramid seems so instinctive because, in its simplest form, it is often the foundation for a *binary plot*, that is, one in which an either/or question is posed near the start of the narrative and answered at the climax or resolution. Who is the murderer? Will the two lovers get together? Will Dorothy ever get back to Kansas?

  - In later lectures, we'll explore many ways to complicate the answers to those questions, but for now, it's important to emphasize that there are ways to complicate this kind of plot long before you get to the end. A binary plot structured according to the Freytag pyramid doesn't have to be a simplistic or unsophisticated one.

  - You can scale up the story to encompass more time and more characters by weaving together several binary plots or Freytag pyramids into one larger narrative. In George Eliot's novel *Middlemarch*, for example, the central story is about a love triangle, but there are also two other major romantic relationships in the book, in addition to several other subplots, each of which follows its own Freytag pyramid.

- Using a *fractal plot* is another way to complicate a traditional narrative structure. A fractal is a kind of self-similar mathematical pattern, meaning that it looks the same at a distance as it does up close.

  - Trees are an excellent example: The limbs of a tree coming off the trunk make the same basic pattern as the branches coming off each limb; the twigs make the same pattern coming off each branch; and so on.

  - You can create the same effect with large-scale narratives, such as novels that run in a series but come to a final conclusion. George R. R. Martin's *A Song of Ice and Fire* poses a single binary question: Who will sit on the Iron Throne and be the king or queen of Westeros? In Martin's work, however, this larger binary plot is made up of a vast number of smaller but no less compelling binary plots at nearly every level.

- Another way to vary the Freytag pyramid is to create *leapfrogging* or a *contrapuntal narrative*.

  o The first variation of this approach tells a single story from the point of view of multiple characters. One famous example is William Faulkner's *As I Lay Dying*, which is narrated from the point of view of 15 different characters, each speaking in the first person.

  o Another variation of leapfrogging is one that tells several equally important stories that remain separate for much of the book but come together at the end for a single climax. J. R. R. Tolkien used this approach in *The Fellowship of the Ring*. At the end of this book, the overarching story of the quest to destroy the Ring of Power splits into three equally important strands that are then followed to the climax of *The Return of the King*.

  o Still another variation of contrapuntal narrative is commonly used by modern historical novelists. Here, two main stories that are linked, one from the past and one from the present, are woven together. An excellent example is A. S. Byatt's novel *Possession*, in which the outcome of the historical plot determines the outcome of the modern one.

  o Finally, the basic murder mystery is usually a contrapuntal story. It's the most basic kind of binary plot there is—who killed the victim?—but the answer is often found through a combination of the present-day story and the story of the recent past.

Suggested Reading

Aristotle, *Poetics*.

Byatt, *Possession*.

Eliot, *Middlemarch*.

Faulkner, *As I Lay Dying*.

Martin, *A Song of Ice and Fire*.

Tolkien, *The Lord of the Rings*.

Writing Exercise

1. Try to graph some of your favorite books, movies, or television shows on Freytag's pyramid. Notice how common this structure is but also how often it is a complicated tangle of many pyramids rather than a single pyramid. If you don't want a traditionally structured plot to become a straightjacket, you need to walk a fine line between being too predictable, on the one hand, and disappointing the reader, on the other. You want readers to be satisfied and not feel betrayed by your climax, but you don't want them to see it coming. This exercise will help you begin to think about meeting that challenge.

Adding Complexity to Plots
Lecture 11

In the last two lectures, we saw that many narratives have the same basic structure, and we saw that varying this structure, such as rearranging the chronology or braiding several plotlines together, can make plotting both interesting and challenging. The fairly large-scale approaches that we've looked at affect the structure of the narrative as a whole, but in this lecture, we'll look at several more focused techniques that can be used on a smaller scale to make a plot more subtle and satisfying. These include suspense, flash-forwards, flashbacks, and foreshadowing. We'll also explore the important topic of withholding information in structuring plots.

Withholding Information and Suspense

- Because plotting seems daunting to many writers, it's important to keep in mind that one of the fundamental principles of plotting is the withholding of information. At the beginning of a plot, you want readers to know very little—just enough to intrigue them—but at the end, you want them to know everything. We might even say that plotting is the mechanism by which the writer decides what information to withhold early on, what information to reveal, and in what order to reveal it.

- Because all books and stories are read over time and can't be imbibed all at once, the most fundamental thing a writer withholds from the reader is how the story ends. In the simplest kind of stories, this is the main reason to keep reading: to find out how it all turns out. But there are other kinds of withholding that result in more subtle plots.

- Consider, for example, Shirley Jackson's well-known story "The Lottery." It's about a small New England village that holds a lottery once a year among all the adult villagers; the person who "wins" the lottery is then stoned to death by the others. The main reason this story works is that Jackson introduces the concept of the lottery in the first paragraph but withholds its purpose from the reader until the end.

- The surprise ending is a fairly simple kind of withholding; yet another kind is the creation of suspense. In a story that involves a surprise, the writer withholds information from the reader and sometimes from the characters, but when a writer creates suspense, he or she generally withholds information from the characters while letting the reader in on the secret.

- Other kinds of withholding have to do with rearranging the elements of the traditional plot; these techniques are perhaps not so much about withholding information as they are about simply presenting it to the reader in an unusual order.

   o As John Gardner points out in *The Art of Fiction*, exposition can take place at any point in the narrative, but in most cases, you want to save a good deal of your exposition for later. At the beginning, you want to say enough about the situation and the major characters to intrigue the reader, but you don't want to explain too much. Parceling out exposition only as needed is an approach that often feels more natural than dropping all the information on the reader's doorstep at once; in many cases, you are providing the information to the reader at the same time that the characters are learning it.

   o In popular fiction, the inciting action—the moment conflict is introduced into the story and gets the plot going—often comes at the very beginning, before the exposition. A good example is the opening of the movie *Jaws*, when a young woman goes for a midnight swim and is eaten by the shark. Only after that do we meet Chief Brody, the first of the three main characters, and learn about the island community of Amity. The traditional elements of the Freytag pyramid are present but in a different order.

   o In fact, you can even structure a story so that you give away the climax in the first few moments, as in James Baldwin's novel *Giovanni's Room*. If we lay out the events of this story in chronological order, the results look like the Freytag pyramid. But Baldwin shrewdly gives us the most dramatic element right at the start, which has the effect of intriguing us, making us want to know exactly how things turned out so badly for the characters who have just been introduced.

Flash-Forwards and Flashbacks

- Both flash-forwards and flashbacks are scenes that take place out of the main chronological order of the story. A flash-forward is a glimpse of something that will happen to the characters in the future, at the end of or perhaps even after the main narrative, and a flashback is a scene that takes place before the main plotline started.

- Flash-forwards are often used in first-person narratives, with the narrator giving the reader a glimpse of an intriguing outcome before returning to the beginning and showing how the story worked its way up to that point. One famous first-person flash-forward is the beginning of Billy Wilder's great film about Hollywood, *Sunset Boulevard*, which opens with the narrator essentially starting his story from beyond the grave.

Many detective stories consist largely of flashbacks as the detective or investigator hears from witnesses about the situation that led up to the murder.

- But using a flash-forward as a teaser to hook the reader at the beginning of a plot can occasionally come across as mechanical. You can use flash-forward elsewhere in a narrative, even at the end, skipping a period of time to show how the characters turn out years after the main chronology of the story. An effective example of this approach is Alice Munro's short story "The Beggar Maid."

- Flashbacks, of course, are much more common. Many detective stories employ flashbacks, but they can also be used to great effect in other genres or in more mainstream fiction. Indeed, flashbacks can often be used as replacements for, or in combination with, exposition, especially when you're trying to present the reader with important or dramatic information about the previous history of a character. Toni Morrison uses this technique to show the dramatic birth of a character in her novel *Beloved.*

Foreshadowing

- A flash-forward is usually a fully evoked and dramatized scene set in the future, but foreshadowing is a hint or a series of hints that a writer plants in the narrative early on to prepare the way for what comes later. In many cases, the success of the narrative's resolution depends on how carefully the writer has prepared the way for it. You want the resolution to be unpredictable but satisfying, and pulling that off requires a balance between withholding information and revealing just enough so that the reader doesn't feel cheated at the end.

- Some foreshadowing is fairly mechanical, such as making sure you introduce all the characters, context, and props you need for a story to pay off. The Russian playwright Anton Chekhov famously said that if you show the audience a pistol on the wall in the first act, then that pistol must go off in the third act. This is a fundamental insight about creating plot.
  - Part of what Chekhov means is simply that you have to play fair with the audience: You can't have a character suddenly waving a pistol around without giving some hint early on that waving a pistol was at least a possibility.

  - But Chekhov is also saying that you need to pay attention to what details you include and when you include them. If you show a pistol on the wall, and nobody uses it, you've set up an expectation in the reader, then thwarted it.

- o Chekhov's rule about the pistol is also an implicit reminder that a plot is not like real life. In our ordinary lives, we see countless details every day, and we decide in the moment, usually subconsciously, what's important and what's not. But a narrative is not like real life: Every detail has a meaning and is included for a specific purpose; you must think about what details are important, what details you can ignore or leave out, and in what order you introduce them.

- One example of foreshadowing is found in Flannery O'Connor's short story "A Good Man Is Hard to Find," about a southern family that encounters a criminal on a road trip to Florida. At the beginning of the story, the family's grandmother tries to talk her son out of going by pointing out a story she's read in the newspaper about a criminal on the loose and headed toward Florida.

  - o The first time you read the story, this episode comes across as nothing more than gentle family comedy, evoking an old woman's groundless paranoia and her son's taciturn refusal to be manipulated.

  - o Indeed, most of the story is a comic account of the family's road trip, complete with bickering children and a colorful episode at a barbecue shack. It isn't until the final few pages, when the family encounters the criminal, that you realize how efficiently detailed and tightly constructed it is. Without that bit of foreshadowing in the first paragraph, the story simply wouldn't have the same effect.

- Another example is found in Joseph Conrad's *Nostromo*, a novel about a revolution in a fictional South American country. An Englishman named Charles Gould owns a silver mine in this country, and in the days before the revolution, he decides to hide his stockpile of silver so that the revolutionaries can't get it. To do this, he puts the silver on a barge, which he entrusts to an Italian sailor named Nostromo and a young journalist named Martin Decoud. They take the silver to an island off the coast to keep it safe from the rebels. In the end, the effect the silver has on Nostromo becomes the central moral dilemma of the book.

o The opening chapter of *Nostromo* is a masterpiece of exposition, consisting mainly of a long, evocative description of this fictional country's geography. In the third paragraph, Conrad relates a local legend about two foreigners who, years ago, ventured onto a remote peninsula in search of some legendary buried gold and were never heard from again. According to the legend, the ghosts of the two foreigners are still guarding the treasure they discovered: "Their souls cannot tear themselves away from their bodies."

Suggested Reading

Baldwin, *Giovanni's Room.*

Conrad, *Nostromo.*

Gardner, *The Art of Fiction.*

Jackson, "The Lottery."

Morrison, *Beloved.*

Munro, "The Beggar Maid."

O'Connor, "A Good Man Is Hard to Find."

Writing Exercise

1. Choose a particular situation and tell it first as a surprise, then as a passage of suspense. If you want to use a ticking bomb, you can, but the scene doesn't have to be violent—in fact, it can be a ticking bomb equivalent. Consider our story from the first lecture about Sarah and Brad. In the surprise version, you might tell it from Brad's point of view, in which case Sarah's announcement that she wants a divorce is as much as a surprise to the reader as it is to Brad. But you might also tell it from Sarah's point of view, in which case the reader would know from the start that she wants a divorce, and the scene becomes one of suspense as we wait anxiously for Brad to learn the truth.

Structuring a Narrative without a Plot
Lecture 12

E very work of fiction has a structure, but not every work of fiction has a plot, at least not a traditional plot. Even if it doesn't have a plot, however, every work of fiction has, or ought to have, something the writer John Gardner called "profluence," which he defined as the feeling that you're getting somewhere when you're reading a work of fiction. Whether or not a story has a plot, something should change over the course of reading it, if not in the story itself, at least in the heart or mind of the reader. In this lecture, we'll explore a few ways to structure fiction that don't involve using the Freytag pyramid or the traditional plot.

Chekhov's "The Kiss"

- The birth of the modern short story took place in the late 19th century with the Russian writer Anton Chekhov. In his story "The Kiss," the officers of an artillery regiment training in the Russian countryside are invited by a local landowner to spend the evening at his country house. During the evening, the main character, a shy officer named Ryabovitch, wanders into a dark room and receives a kiss from a woman who has mistaken him for someone else.

  o The woman flees the room, and Ryabovitch is unable to discover who kissed him. For days afterward, Ryabovitch fantasizes about the encounter, inventing a whole future life with this woman, even though he doesn't know who she is.

  o At the end of the story, when his regiment returns to the same town and the landowner invites the officers back to his house, Ryabovitch loses his nerve and stays behind in the barracks.

- "The Kiss" reads like a conventional story; the scenes are laid out in chronological order, with no flashbacks or flash-forwards. Yet the story doesn't come to a climax or resolve in the same way as a traditional story. Ryabovitch does not develop as a character. He has a brief glimpse of a more exciting life, but his only response is in his lonely imagination, and he does nothing about it.

- The genius of the story is not so much that it's plotless as that it suggests a potential conflict, then refuses to resolve it. Chekhov sets up a binary question—who kissed Ryabovitch, and will he ever find her again?—and technically, he answers the question—no, Ryabovitch won't find the girl. That disappointment is the point of the story: The real question is not whether Ryabovitch gets the girl, but whether he can rise above his own timid nature; that is a much more profound and unsettling question.

- Even though nothing "happens" in "The Kiss" in the traditional sense, something profound changes over the course of the story—not in the character or the situation but in the reader.

Joyce's "The Dead"
- "The Dead" is the final story in James Joyce's only volume of short fiction, *Dubliners*. Instead of a conventional climax or resolution, the stories in this book rely on what Joyce called an *epiphany*. In religious terms, the word *epiphany* means a deep spiritual insight or realization brought about by divine intervention; Joyce used it to refer to an individual experiencing a moment of profound, sometimes life-changing, self-understanding.

- "The Dead" is the longest story in *Dubliners*, and like "The Kiss," it reads conventionally; it's a chronological account of a party in Dublin in January 1904. Most of the story is told from the point of view of a successful middle-aged man named Gabriel Conroy. Near the end of the party, Gabriel witnesses his wife, Gretta, listening raptly to a singer performing an old Irish folksong.
    o In the cab on the way to the hotel room they've booked for the night, Gabriel experiences a powerful lust for his wife, but when they're alone in the room, he realizes that Gretta is upset. She tells him that hearing the folksong at the party has reminded her of a boy named Michael Furey who loved her when she was a young woman. Furey used to sing the same

song to her, and he probably died because he stood in the rain, waiting outside her window.

   o   Gabriel realizes that to make love to his wife at this moment would be akin to an assault; thus, after she falls asleep, he simply lies awake in the dark next to her. Gabriel's epiphany is his realization that Gretta has never loved him as much she loved Furey, and he further realizes that he has never loved her, or anyone else, the way Furey loved Gretta. But instead of feeling rage or disappointment, Gabriel experiences a moment of expansive generosity for his wife, for himself, for Furey, and in Joyce's famous phrase, for all the living and the dead.

- You might think that Joyce could have evoked Gabriel's epiphany in a shorter story, one that focused only on the aftermath of the party, but that simply wouldn't have worked.
   o   The first 40 pages of the story, a chronological account of the party, are structurally essential to Joyce's purpose. Not only does he include details about Gabriel that pay off only at the end, but he shows us how a long-married couple present themselves to their friends and acquaintances in a public setting. This makes their moment of unexpected intimacy at the end even more poignant and piercing.

   o   We need to see, at length and in detail, the life that Gabriel thought he was living in order to understand his shock when he realizes that nothing he thought about his life was true.

- At first glance, the structure of "The Dead" is similar to that of "The Kiss." Both are chronological, both are centered on a party, and both are essentially a series of evocative scenes that do not make up a conventional plot. The final effect of "The Dead," however, is different from that of the "The Kiss" because Gabriel comes to a new understanding of himself and Ryabovitch does not.

- Think back to the distinction E. M. Forster made between a story and plot: that a story tells us what happened, but a plot tells us why. Then think back to how a conventional plot does this: by posing a question in the form of a conflict, then answering the question by resolving the conflict.

    o The structural brilliance of "The Dead" is that it does not set up a conflict at the start of the story; instead, it holds your interest by giving you a plotless but entertaining account of its main character and his social situation; it then blindsides you at the end with a conflict that neither you nor the main character even knew existed.

    o The conclusion of "The Dead" is powerful partly because of what it says—that happiness is rare and precarious and sometimes founded on a lie—but it's also powerful because of the way Joyce plays with our expectations. He gives us what looks like an ordinary day for its main character, then surprises both Gabriel and the reader with something extraordinary.

Woolf's *Mrs. Dalloway*

- The use of everyday moments to build a picture of a world at a particular moment in order to reveal something profound also lies behind Virginia Woolf's novel *Mrs. Dalloway*. The novel is set over a single day in London in the early 1920s and focuses on a 52-year-old woman named Clarissa Dalloway as she prepares for a party at her home that evening. Other major characters include

© Maria Teijeiro/Digital Vision/Thinkstock.

Virginia Woolf's stream-of-consciousness technique in *Mrs. Dalloway* requires more concentration than following a conventional plot, but it provides a more vivid evocation of a particular moment in time in the lives of the characters.

Peter Walsh, a former suitor of Clarissa's who has just returned from five years' service in India, and Septimus Warren Smith, a veteran of World War I who is suffering from shell-shock.

- There are only a few conventionally dramatic moments in *Mrs. Dalloway*, including the suicide of Septimus Smith and the meeting of Clarissa and Peter Walsh after many years, as well as a few flashbacks. Except for the death of Septimus, it's a fairly unremarkable day.

- Given that there's no conflict, no climax, and nothing to resolve at the end, what gives the book its structure? Instead of using a plot to structure the novel, Woolf uses two techniques, one of which governs the overall shape of the novel, and the other, its movement within and between scenes.

  o The overall shape comes from the fact that the novel is set over the course of one day, which allows Woolf to limit the number of incidents in the book and the scope of the characters.

  o The technique Woolf uses to make the novel flow from moment to moment is stream of consciousness. As you recall, when we read the passage in which Clarissa looks in a shop window, her thoughts shifted quickly and subtly from the world around her to her memories of girlhood, the last days of her uncle, and her relationship with her daughter. Each brief moment in that passage tells us something about Clarissa that we didn't know before. In other words, it is profluent enough without Clarissa having to confront or resolve a conflict.

- Perhaps the most remarkable feature of *Mrs. Dalloway* is the way Woolf effortlessly, often suddenly, shifts the narrative's point of view among a number of characters. These shifts also provide the sort of narrative momentum that other, more conventional books rely on plot to provide. They enable Woolf to evoke a particular moment in time and in the lives of her characters far more vividly than in a conventionally plotted narrative.

Postmodernist Techniques

- In this lecture, we've seen several ways to structure a piece of fiction that don't rely on a plot with a conflict and a resolution. Obviously, the techniques we've explored are not for everyone; most writers fall back on plot because it's easy and it's what most readers expect and enjoy. But trying to write a story or a book with an unconventional technique can make you a more observant, subtle, and engaged writer, even if you then go back and apply what you've learned to a more conventional narrative.

- The type of fiction known as *postmodernism* is even more adventurous than the modernist works we've explored in this lecture. In general, a postmodern novel is one that calls attention to itself as a novel, plays games with language and with narrative conventions of plot and character, and constantly calls attention to the fact that it is a work of fiction.

- Even if you have no interest in writing this kind of fiction yourself, it's worth looking into some of the stories and books of postmodernism, including David Foster Wallace's *Infinite Jest*, Roger Boylan's *Killoyle*, Jennifer Egan's *A Visit from the Goon Squad*, and Kate Atkinson's *Life after Life*.

Suggested Reading

Chekhov, "The Kiss."

Joyce, "The Dead."

Woolf, *Mrs. Dalloway*.

Writing Exercise

1. Choose a single character and write about an hour in that person's life, limiting yourself to five pages. Don't pick the hour when something significant happened to the character—when he or she committed a murder or fell in love, for example. Instead, pick one of the countless hours in a person's life where nothing particularly important is going on. But try to put in as much detail about that person as you can, including memories or flashbacks that might be provoked by something as simple as a smell or an overheard comment. By limiting the time period and the number of pages, you provide yourself with a structure that doesn't rely on plot, but if you include significant detail, you may be pleasantly surprised at how much you can get across about the character.

In the Beginning—How to Start a Plot
Lecture 13

Getting a plot started is a daunting prospect for most writers, but the reason it's daunting varies from writer to writer. Some writers know so much about the story even before they start that they don't quite know where to begin. Others have only a single episode or character in mind, and they're not sure how to spin that situation into a complete narrative. In this lecture, we'll explore three ways to work a writer works out plot, outlined by John Gardner: "by borrowing some traditional plot or an action from real life ... by working his way back from the story's climax; or by groping his way forward from an initial situation."

Working out Plots

- Gardner's first method of approaching plot is borrowing, but it's important to note that this is not the same as plagiarism, which generally involves passing off someone else's work as your own. Borrowing, in contrast, usually involves changing an earlier plot in significant ways or using it for a purpose that the original author may not have intended or even foreseen. Many writers, for example, have retold Homer's *Odyssey*, setting it in completely different contexts. Others have retold well-known stories from a different point of view.

  o Of course, historical novels take their stories from famous people or events in history. As with novels that adapt earlier works of literature, the best historical novels reimagine history in interesting ways. For example, Robert Graves's novel *I, Claudius* and Marguerite Yourcenar's *The Memoirs of Hadrian* each tell the story of a Roman emperor from the emperor's point of view.

  o Sometimes, writers borrow types of plots rather than specific stories. Beginning writers of mysteries or romance novels, for example, probably have templates for those sorts of stories in their minds. Although such a template can be a straightjacket, it can also be a convenient way to at least get a plot started, even if you plan to change it later on.

- o And sometimes writers borrow a plot when they need to provide a structure for the material that truly interests them. The science fiction writer William Gibson structured his first novel, *Neuromancer*, as an old-fashioned noir thriller in the style of Dashiell Hammett or Raymond Chandler. He was interested in evoking a rich, complex, and colorful future and in playing with the cultural, social, and political implications of the computer revolution; thus, he used a thriller plot to provide a framework for this material.

- Another approach to plotting is to start with the end of a story and structure the rest of the work so that it leads to a particular climax. Obviously, this method requires that you know how the story ends before you start writing. It also probably works best if you're writing a binary narrative, that is, one with an either/or conclusion.
  - o With this type of narrative, figuring out how to start by working backward should be relatively easy: If there's a crime to be solved, you start with the crime or its immediate aftermath; if the two lovers finally get together, you need to start with their meeting or the situation that leads to their meeting.

  - o This is the method where you're most likely to find that an outline is useful. If you already know what happens at the end, that means you know, or at least can infer, what the plot needs to do to reach that point: what characters you'll need, what the setting will be, and roughly what steps the characters need to take to get there.

- Finally, many writers start with an image, a character, or a situation and, as Gardner put it, "grope" their way forward. William Faulkner famously said that he created his great novel *The Sound and the Fury* by starting with a single image of a little girl with muddy underpants sitting in a tree, peering through a window at a funeral. This method is probably more time-consuming and frustrating than sticking to an outline, but it may result in a more complex narrative structure.

- The methods of structuring a plot are not limited to these three, of course, and the methods can be combined in interesting ways. Even if you're borrowing a plot, you may find yourself monkeying with it, and even if you're trying to stick to the facts of a famous life—such as the life of Hadrian or Copernicus—it's what you discover in the process of writing, as you imagine yourself into their minds, that makes the narrative come alive.

Starting *in Medias Res*
- As mentioned in an earlier lecture, many stories begin *in medias res*, "in the middle of things." In fact, it's tempting to say that all stories begin *in medias res* because there's really no such thing as a story that begins *ex nihilo*, "from nothing." Even if you start a novel with the birth of the main character, that character already has parents and relations, a family history, and a social and historical context.

- What *in medias res* usually means is starting the plot at a point where the story is already underway. Homer's *Iliad* is not really about the Trojan War in its entirety; by the time the *Iliad* opens, the war has already been going on for 10 years, and the present-time narrative depicts only a few weeks near the end of the siege of Troy. Even though it makes reference to how the war began and how it ends, the *Iliad* does not dramatize the kidnapping of Helen, which started the war, or the fall of Troy, which ended it.

- Starting *in medias res* shows us that choosing where to begin is not so much a matter of figuring out the chronological beginning of a story as it is choosing the most dramatically productive moment. Shakespeare could have started *Hamlet* with the funeral of Hamlet's father or the subsequent marriage of Hamlet's mother to his uncle Polonius, but he chose to open it with the moment that was most likely to make Hamlet reconsider recent events, namely, the appearance of his father's ghost, demanding vengeance.

Limiting Choices

- Another way to approach the start of a plot is to limit your choices. As we've mentioned, real life flows ceaselessly and infinitely in all directions; it's knowing what to leave out that turns life into fiction. Thus, you could limit your time frame, having the story or novel take place in a single day, week, or month, or you could limit the point of view, telling the story from the point of view of only one character.
    - Neither of these limits necessarily means that you have to leave out other settings or other times in the characters' lives.

    - You can start the narrative at a particular moment and limit it to particular time, the way Virginia Woolf limits *Mrs. Dalloway* to the events of one day, yet still range backward and forward in time and place, incorporating flashback scenes that take place at other times and in different settings.

- You also have a number of choices with the first line of a narrative, which will both dictate and be dictated by what comes later.
    - If you're telling a story from the point of view of a character who dies at the end, for example, you will be limited to third-person narration—unless you want the character to narrate the story from beyond the grave. If you're writing a story that features a surprise later on, you might want to start in the first person present tense or in the close third person, so that the reader lives in the moment right alongside the main character and is just as stunned as the character when the surprise finally comes.

    - Look at the openings of books and stories you admire, paying attention to not just the immediate effect of the opening moment but also how the opening prepares the reader for what comes later.

Opening Examples

- One category of story opening is simply beginning at the beginning, the way Tolkien does in *The Hobbit*: "In a hole in the ground there lived a hobbit." This opening sounds like the beginning of a fairy tale, with an unspoken "once upon a time" at the start of the sentence. As brief and to the point as it is, that simple 10-word sentence tells us right away that we're in a fantasy world, inhabited by creatures called hobbits, and it tells us something important about hobbits, that they live underground.

- Another way to begin at the beginning is simply to state the premise of the story as bluntly as possible, the way Franz Kafka does in the first line of his story "The Metamorphosis": "One morning, upon awakening from agitated dreams, Gregor Samsa found himself, in his bed, transformed into a monstrous vermin." This sentence is only 19 words, but at the end of it, we know the name of the main character, that he is a man ridden with anxieties, and that he has undergone a horrific transformation. The rest of the story works out all the implications of a man being transformed overnight into a giant cockroach.

- Both of those openings are in the third person, but many of the most famous American novels begin with a first-person narrator speaking directly to the reader. Herman Melville's *Moby-Dick* begins with "Call me Ishmael," and Mark Twain's *The Adventures of Huckleberry Finn* begins with "You don't know about me, without you have read a book by the name of *The Adventures of Tom Sawyer*, but that ain't no matter."

- As we've said, writing is about imposing order on chaos, about making decisions—often arbitrary ones—out of what seems to be an infinity of choices. It's also as much about what you leave out as what you leave in. Your decision about when, where, and with whom to begin a narrative opens one path for you even as it closes off many others.
    - Just like making decisions in real life, you sometimes don't realize what the consequences of your choices are until much later. But unlike life, if you find you've made a wrong decision about the opening of your novel or short story, you can always go back and change it or even start over.

    - Writing, especially plotting, is not a science; it's an organic and wildly inefficient process of trial and error. But it's the stuff you don't plan for, the stuff that surprises you, that makes fiction worth reading and makes the writing of it simultaneously frustrating and rewarding.

Suggested Reading

Faulkner, *The Sound and the Fury*.

Gardner, *The Art of Fiction*.

Hynes, *Next*.

Kafka, "The Metamorphosis."

Robinson, *Housekeeping*.

Tolkien, *The Hobbit*.

Writing Exercise

1. Without thinking about it too much, imagine some sort of striking or intriguing situation. For example, imagine a man and woman who are eating at a candlelit table in a romantic restaurant, but they aren't speaking to each other; in fact, they don't even look at each other. Or imagine a woman standing in an alley in the rain at night, holding a knife. Then, again without thinking about it too much, try imagining the very next thing that happens, then the next, and the next. If you find yourself running out of steam or boxing yourself into a corner, go back to the original situation and try something completely different.

Happily Ever After—How to End a Plot
Lecture 14

If starting a narrative is daunting, bringing one to an end can be tricky. What readers think of the end of a plot often colors their opinions of the entire narrative. A plot that has a successful or, at least, a vivid ending can make a mediocre narrative seem better than it is, while a weak ending can make an otherwise superb narrative lose its luster. Endings are also difficult because what people consider a good ending depends on individual taste and because what writers and readers consider a good ending has changed over time. In this lecture, however, we'll look at two fundamental qualities that nearly everyone agrees an ending should have: believability and satisfaction.

Believability and Satisfaction
- In part, believability depends on what we as readers bring to a story, specifically our own individual understanding of how the real world works and what real people are like.
  - This doesn't mean that the rules of the real world can't be bent: Your readers are willing to accept that the laws of nature can be altered, broken, or ignored in fantasy, horror, and science fiction, as long as you provide an alternative set of rules for your fictional world and stick to them.

  - Readers of any genre, however, are less likely to buy into a character whose final actions violate their beliefs about human psychology. Different readers have different ideas and expectations about how human beings think and behave or how they ought to think or behave. An ending that strikes one reader as completely plausible and even admirable may strike another as preposterous and even offensive.

- Consider the ending of *Jane Eyre*. The brooding, sexually magnetic Mr. Rochester persuades Jane to fall in love with him without bothering to tell her that he's already married and that he keeps his first wife locked in the attic. At the end of the novel, after a series of plot twists, Jane happily marries Mr. Rochester.

- Most readers accept this ending, given the narrative conventions of the time and because Jane is such an admirable character that we want her to be happy. Still, it's possible to imagine a reader who just can't believe that someone as smart and independent as Jane would give someone as manipulative and self-serving as Mr. Rochester a second chance.

- If you believe that character is more fundamental to fiction than plot, then the key to crafting a believable ending is staying true to the nature of your characters. You can make an ending believable if you can get the reader to play along with the premise and if you play fair with the reader by obeying the rules of your own world but especially by respecting your own characters.

- Just because an ending is believable doesn't mean it's satisfying. In the terminology of philosophy, believability is a necessary condition of a satisfying ending, but it is not a sufficient one.

- As we've seen, believability isn't an absolute quality, but satisfaction is even more dependent on taste and personal experience.

- We can conceivably make a case for the believability of an ending, but we can no more convince a skeptic to be satisfied by an ending than we can make people change their minds about foods they don't like.

Resolution

- In *The Art of Fiction*, John Gardner says that there are two ways a narrative can end: "in resolution, when no further event can take place … or in logical exhaustion." Of course, there are other types of endings, but these two definitions probably cover most possibilities. Let's start with resolution, which is what we've termed a binary ending—one that resolves an either/or situation or answers a simple question posed at the beginning of the narrative.

- Plots with binary endings are often dismissed as mechanical and contrived, and many of them are. We could even argue that the ending of some simple binary narratives is the least important thing about them; the real reason we enjoy them is that we enjoy the setting or characters. This is often the case with well-written genre narratives: The journey is interesting, even if the destination turns out to be unmemorable.

Binary endings are the kind we find in most bestselling novels and popular movies and television shows: Who committed the crime? Will the star-crossed lovers get together?

- But it's also true that many binary endings are both immensely satisfying and unforgettable, perhaps even the high point of the story.

  o John le Carré's novel *Tinker, Tailor, Soldier, Spy* is the story of a veteran British spy named George Smiley who is asked by the British intelligence service to find a Soviet mole in its midst.

  o Le Carré complicates the ending of the novel by making the mole an upper-class Englishman and a former lover of Smiley's wife. It's a binary ending with layers, because the mole's betrayal is at once political, social, and personal.

- Many literary novels also have binary endings. Perhaps the most satisfying binary ending of a literary story can be found in Henry James's *The Aspern Papers*. Here, James not only imagines a binary situation that generates suspense, but he peoples the plot with three vivid and sharply defined characters and stays true to them throughout.

Logical Exhaustion

- Gardner's "logical exhaustion" is the point at which a narrative has reached its deepest understanding of a character or a situation, beyond which it would just be repeating itself. This sort of ending does not rely on raising a binary expectation in the reader, but it does require the early pages to draw the reader into the narrative, setting up an expectation that some sort of revelation will occur.

- One variety of this kind of ending is the epiphany, exemplified in Katherine Mansfield's short story "Miss Brill." Like many epiphany stories, this one doesn't have a plot, but like the best of them, it is carefully constructed to deliver a devastating emotional blow at the end.
  - o Every sharply observed detail and every slight shift of emotion in this story builds toward a single piercing epiphany. Mansfield starts by introducing a late-middle-aged woman who lives alone and whose most elegant possession is an old fox stole, which reminds her of her youth.

  - o In the middle section, Mansfield shows us the park Miss Brill visits every Sunday and allows us to participate in what she sees there. We see how she prides herself on her gift of quiet observation, and we share the slight superiority she feels toward the people she observes so sharply.

  - o We share Miss Brill's moment of communion with the people in the park: She's one of the players in a kind of play they all put on each Sunday. She even takes a brief respite from her loneliness by indulging in the fantasy of them all singing together. But then, her illusions are shattered by two thoughtless lovers who sit on the end of her park bench, and in the end, she sees herself as the world sees her—old, unfashionable, and alone.

  - o There's no binary plot here, no situation to resolve, but the story moves with ruthless efficiency to an ending that's every bit as precision engineered—and every bit as powerful—as the ending of *The Aspern Papers*.

Hybrid Ending
- The hybrid ending exists halfway between the binary ending and the epiphany. We see an example in Flannery O'Connor's story "A Good

Man Is Hard to Find," about a southern family that takes a drive to Florida and ends up murdered on a lonely country road by a serial killer.

- The killer, who is called The Misfit, is mentioned in the first paragraph of the story, when the grandmother of the family reads aloud from the newspaper about his recent escape from prison. Then, The Misfit is mentioned only once more, briefly, in the middle of the narrative, before he and his henchmen turn up later.

- The reappearance of The Misfit might have been a Dickensian coincidence in the hands of a lesser writer, but his appearance in the newspaper in the first paragraph is played for laughs so that when he reappears at the end full of genuine menace, the reader's experience mirrors that of the family members as they slowly realize that they're about to die.

- The ending of "A Good Man Is Hard to Find" falls halfway between a binary ending and an epiphany. On the one hand, it ends definitively, with the murder of several of its characters, but like an epiphany story, it changes everything the reader thought about what came before. It doesn't answer a question that was openly posed at the beginning of the story but instead answers a question that the reader didn't even realize was being posed until the story is finished: Is the world a safe place? O'Connor answers with a definitive no.

Thoughts on Endings
- The endings of "A Good Man Is Hard to Find," *The Aspern Papers*, and "Miss Brill" are all satisfying in part because they are all prepared for early in the narrative. All three of these endings also essentially leave the reader with nothing left to know. The major questions are answered, and we have gained our deepest understanding of the situation or the characters.

- The fact that all three of these endings are more or less airtight and perfectly prepared for doesn't necessarily mean that James, Mansfield, and O'Connor knew the ending of each story before he or she started.
  - It might seem that knowing the ending in advance is the easiest way to write, because you can craft the story to head in that

direction. But you may also find yourself forcing the characters in a particular direction whether they want to go there or not, with the result that your plot can seem contrived and your characters can seem more like puppets than real people.

o Not knowing where you're going may sometimes be easier than planning ahead and may even lead to a more satisfying ending. You may find that your ending arises effortlessly and organically from the situation and the characters—an inevitable result of your choices along the way. Of course, with this method, you may also find that you have painted yourself into a corner or drafted a narrative that just peters out.

• We've noted repeatedly that literature is the creation of meaning out of an otherwise meaningless existence. The ending of a narrative is where that meaning is most sharply defined. It's where the hidden patterns are finally revealed, and we at last have a moment, however fleeting, where we understand everything that came before. In other words, the secret of a satisfying ending is not that it's definitive or revelatory, happy or unhappy, but that there's nothing left to say.

Suggested Reading

Forster, *Aspects of the Novel.*

James, *The Aspern Papers.*

Mansfield, "Miss Brill."

O'Connor, "A Good Man Is Hard to Find."

1. Choose a story or a novel that you love, imagine a different ending for it, and then work backward to see what you'd have to change to make the new ending believable and satisfying. Consider *Jane Eyre* as an example. Jot down a rough outline of everything in the book that leads to Jane's marriage to Mr. Rochester, then imagine a different ending: She marries someone else in the novel, or she decides to live by herself on her inheritance money. Go back through your outline to see what you'd have to change in the story to make the new ending work.

Seeing through Other Eyes—Point of View
Lecture 15

A s we've seen throughout these lectures, writing fiction is all about making choices, and deciding what point of view and voice to adopt in a narrative is one of the most important choices you have to make. This choice not only determines the perspective from which the story and plot are viewed, but it can determine what actually happens, and it has a powerful effect on what characters you include and how you depict them. In this lecture, we'll take a quick tour of the most important types of point of view; then, in the next two lectures, we'll look at the first person point of view and the third person point of view in more detail.

Point-of-View Tour

- If you imagine your story as a landscape, you can think of point of view as the dome of the sky arching over the story. The different possible points of view are points on that curve: from the highest point, overlooking the entire landscape, to the lowest point, where a character or a narrator can see only what's directly in front of him or her.

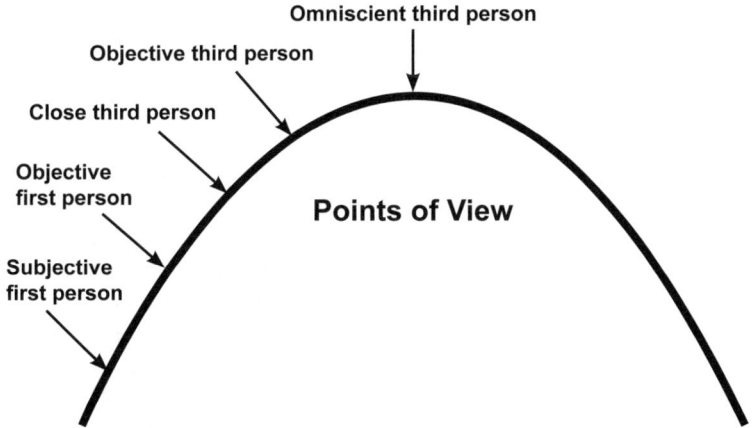

- The most all-inclusive point of view is the omniscient third person. This is the point of view in which the author and the narrator seem to be more or less the same person, though that's not necessarily the case. This sort of narration sees, knows, and usually reveals everything about the characters in the story. This point of view is often called godlike because, like an all-powerful, all-knowing deity, the narration can see into the hearts and minds of its characters, revealing their most intimate secrets.

- A little closer to the ground but still fairly high up on the curve is the objective third-person point of view. One of the best examples of this point of view is Dashiell Hammett's *The Maltese Falcon*. In this novel, although we see and hear everything every character does, we never get inside their minds.

  o Unlike an omniscient point of view, which generally shows us what characters are thinking and feeling, the objective third person is more like a video camera, recording and reporting everything it sees but allowing readers to make up their own minds about the characters' feelings, thought, and motivations.

  o This may be the most lifelike point of view because it reproduces what it feels like for each of us to move through the real world, trying to infer what other people around us are thinking from their speech or actions but never really knowing for sure. Although it's perhaps more lifelike, it's also colder than third-person omniscient, which engages more deeply and intimately in the lives of its characters.

- About halfway down the dome of our imaginary sky is the close or limited third-person point of view. More recently, this has come to be known as *free indirect discourse*. In this point of view, the narration uses third-person pronouns, and like the omniscient third person, it gets inside the minds of its characters. But in many narratives of this sort, the whole story or novel is generally told from the point of view of only one character.

  o Because this close third-person point of view can often shift among several characters in the same narrative, it can easily turn into the omniscient third person. George Eliot's *Middlemarch* is written in this way, as is Faulkner's *Light in August*.

o The traditional omniscient third person is often more remote from its characters and capable of making sweeping judgments about society, whereas modern novels written in the more intimate close third person generally shy away from that.

o Still, the close third person allows the author occasionally to pull back the camera and either comment directly on the action as the author or show us something the point-of-view character can't or doesn't know. Free indirect discourse is the default mode of much contemporary fiction.

- In the objective first person, the narration uses first-person pronouns, but it maintains a certain distance from the action of the narrative. In other words, the story or novel is narrated by a fictional character who plays only a minor part in the story or isn't present in the story at all. Two good examples are Ishmael in *Moby-Dick* and Nick Carraway in *The Great Gatsby*.

- At ground level in our landscape is the subjective first person, in which the first-person narrator is the main character or one of the main characters in the story. For example, Huck Finn is both the narrator and the main character of Mark Twain's *The Adventures of Huckleberry Finn*. We see and hear everything in the book through Huck's eyes, and we know only what Huck witnesses or hears about. In more recent times, the subjective first person has become more prevalent.

- This curve of sky representing different points of view is a continuum, of course, and narratives can and do find points between the ones we've just described. In addition, many books mix and match points of view.

The Narrator's Audience
- One question related to point of view is this: Is the narration addressed to an unknown reader in the real world, or is it addressed to some person or group of people who exist in the world of the story?

- Consider, for example, three of the most famous first-person narratives in literature: Brontë's *Jane Eyre*, Twain's *The Adventures of Huckleberry*

Finn, and Nabokov's *Lolita*. In all three, there are at least hints of the narrator's awareness that he or she is addressing the reader of the book.

o   Jane Eyre narrates her story as if she were writing her memoir for posterity. In the most famous line from the book, she makes it clear that she knows she's writing a book when she says about Mr. Rochester, "Reader, I married him." This is a memorable example of a fictional character speaking directly to the real readers of her book.

o   Huck Finn bridges the gap between fiction and reality in his first sentence: "You don't know about me without you have read a book called *The Adventures of Tom Sawyer* by Mr. Mark Twain." Here, we have a fictional character speaking directly to the reader and referencing a real book by a real author, in which he, Huck, first appears as a fictional character.

o   *Lolita* opens with an introduction by a fictional psychiatrist, and the rest of the book is pitched as a confession written by Humbert Humbert in prison. Unlike Jane Eyre and Huck Finn, who cross the divide between the fictional world and the real world, Humbert Humbert remains more constrained within the pages of his book because he knows he's writing something that may only ever be read by the authorities who locked him away.

• This question becomes even more complicated when we consider first-person narrators who speak in the present tense. Such a narration contributes to the pace and immediacy of an exciting story, but there's something fundamentally improbable about it: Are we to understand that the character is silently narrating his or her own actions in the moment?

• The uses of the third person can be just as diverse. The 19th-century third-person omniscient voice of George Eliot and Leo Tolstoy is very much a public, authoritative voice. The more feverish voice of Dickens, however, sounds more like a particular person, even though he often writes in the third person.

- There are also third-person narrations that presume the reader's intimacy with the social setting and the worldview of the author, such as Jane Austen in *Pride and Prejudice.*

- In the 20th century, the stream-of-consciousness third person of such books as *Mrs. Dalloway* doesn't seem as though it's speaking to anyone outside of the character, let alone outside of the novel. Even though the novel is technically in the third person, the effect of reading *Mrs. Dalloway*'s narrative voice is like eavesdropping on each character's thoughts as they happen.

Temporal Distance

- The other element of point of view and voice that we need to consider is the distance in time from which the story is told. Partly, this is simply a matter of verb tense, but it's also about a larger issue, namely, the distance of the first-person narrator or the third-person narrative voice from the events being depicted.

- With a first-person narrator, you have to decide just how close the narrator is to the events he or she is describing. Huck Finn is told mainly in the past tense, but the implication of Huck's voice throughout the book is that he is still a boy, telling us about a series of events that have happened in the recent past. In other words, it's a story about a child told by the child.

- We get a slightly different effect from Harper Lee's *To Kill a Mockingbird*, where the distance of Scout, the first-person narrator of the novel, is deliberately ambiguous. At times, her narration is immediate and limited to what she knew as a young girl, but the novel also steps back and narrates the events from the point of view of Scout as a grown woman, looking back on her childhood. We get a child's-eye view of childhood leavened with an adult's retrospective explanation of events that Scout as a child wouldn't have fully understood.

- This element of temporal distance from the events in the narrative is just as important with third-person narratives. Being the default tense of so many narratives, the past tense doesn't necessarily mean the distant past:

Tolstoy's *Anna Karenina* is told in the past tense, for example, but it was both written and set during the 1870s. George Eliot's *Middlemarch*, on the other hand, was published in the early 1870s but set 40 years earlier, in the 1830s. Tolstoy uses the past tense to tell a contemporary story, while Eliot uses the past tense to tell a story of the recent past, giving the reader some distance from the events.

o   The 40-year timespan may not seem like much, but if we transfer the difference to the present day, we can see that Eliot's use of the past tense is significantly different from Tolstoy's.

o   Consider the difference between watching the two television shows *Breaking Bad* and *Mad Men*: *Breaking Bad* was set more or less in the present moment, allowing no temporal distance between the story and the viewers. But with *Mad Men*, set in the early 1960s, we can at least cling to the illusion that we are better behaved than the people who worked on Madison Avenue were at that time.

Suggested Reading

Brontë, *Jane Eyre*.

Eliot, *Middlemarch*.

Fitzgerald, *The Great Gatsby*.

Lee, *To Kill a Mockingbird*.

Melville, *Moby-Dick*.

Nabokov, *Lolita*.

Robinson, *Housekeeping*.

Tolstoy, *Anna Karenina*.

Twain, *The Adventures of Huckleberry Finn*.

1. Choose an opening from one of the books discussed in this lecture, another book you've read, or something you've written and try rewriting it from a different point of view, in a different verb tense, or in a different voice. Would *The Adventures of Huckleberry Finn* work if it were narrated in the third person or in the first person by an elderly Huck looking back on his childhood? Would George Eliot be able to create as broad a portrait of the community in *Middlemarch* if it were narrated by only one character? What would *I, Claudius* feel like if it was written in the present tense? Would it make the Roman emperor's court feel more immediate, or would it just feel bizarre?

I, Me, Mine—First-Person Point of View
Lecture 16

T
he inherent improbability of first-person narration was summed up by Henry James in the preface to one of his novels, when he remarked how strange it was to make a first-person narrator both "hero and historian" of his own story. In other words, first-person narration can be peculiar because it often (though not always) must accomplish two goals at once: tell the story and evoke one of the story's characters, often the most important character. But it's also true that first-person narration can be one of the most intimate, seductive, and natural-seeming ways to tell a story. In this lecture, we'll look at several varieties of the first-person narrator and how you can use each of them.

Objective First Person

- The objective first-person narrator is present in the story but is not the most important character. This kind of narration is halfway between the close third person and a more intimate first person.

- One of the most obvious examples of objective first-person narration is Ishmael in *Moby-Dick*. Ishmael, of course, introduces himself in the first line of the novel, and for much of the book, we hear a great deal about his experiences. But the book is more about Captain Ahab than it is about anyone else, and indeed, Ahab and many of the other characters are more interesting than Ishmael. Further, Ismael doesn't develop in the way that characters in modern novels often do.

- In *The Great Gatsby*, Nick Carraway takes much more of a role in the story than Ishmael does, but on the whole, he serves mainly as a recording eye. He is also an outsider to the world he depicts; thus, he's able to record the story of the wealthy characters around him with more objectivity and distance than Gatsby or Daisy could.

- The slightly remote first-person narration allows readers to feel that they are witnessing the events of the novel firsthand but with no pressure to endorse a particular opinion of any of the characters or actions in the story.

  o A version of *Moby-Dick* narrated by Ahab or a version of *The Great Gatsby* narrated by Gatsby would require us to take sides for or against the narrator, while an objective third-person version of these two novels would not be nearly as engaging.

  o Objective first-person narration is especially effective when the central character—as opposed to the narrator—is both charismatic and slippery, as Ahab and Gatsby are. Ishmael and Nick Carraway allow us to get close but not too close.

The Heroic Narrator
- The heroic narrator is usually the main character or one of the main characters and takes an active role in the events of the story. In this case, the narration's evocation of character is equally important to telling the story.

- Both objective first-person and heroic narration invite readers to take the narrator at face value and assume that he or she is telling the truth. But heroic narration also invites readers to actively endorse the narrator's judgments of the other characters and situations in the story.

- We don't root for Nick Carraway in *The Great Gatsby* because he's not the main character, and Nick's slight remove from the action enables us to make up our own minds about Gatsby. But in *Jane Eyre*, we are not only asked to assume that Jane is telling the truth throughout, but we are also actively encouraged to endorse Jane's judgments of the other characters and to root for things to turn out well for her.

- With a heroic narrator, there is not much difference between the narrator's opinion of the other characters and the author's. Consider Philip Marlowe, the hard-boiled private investigator who is the main character and narrator of the detective stories of Raymond Chandler.

At first glance, it might seem as if Marlowe is just a recording-eye narrator, but if we listen to his voice carefully, we realize that he is passing judgment on a world that doesn't share his strict sense of morality.

- A more complex version of the heroic narrator is Huck Finn, a classic example of the *double consciousness* of a first-person narrator. With this technique, a skilled writer can simultaneously

The distance between the author's view of the world and that of the heroic narrator, such as Raymond Chandler's Philip Marlowe, is not very great, allowing both the author and the reader to live through the narrator.

evoke the beliefs and prejudices of his narrator while letting the reader see through the narration to what's really going on.

  o This double consciousness manifests itself at the moral climax of Huck's book, when he must decide whether to allow Jim to be sold back into slavery or to help Jim gain his freedom. Everything about the moral code of Huck's world tells him that letting a slave run away is a kind of theft, and Huck truly believes that sanctioning this theft will send him to hell. But then, he recalls the way he and Jim looked after each other as they floated down the river, and he says, "All right, then, I'll *go* to hell."

  o In this episode, Twain allows us to revel in hearing Huck's reasoning in his unique voice—staying true to the character— but Twain himself also peeks through the character, letting readers know that Huck is doing the right thing, even if Huck doesn't know it for himself.

The Retrospective Narrator
- With retrospective narration, the narrator recalls events from a distance of many years, looking back on a time when he or she was younger. In

this type of narration, there is also an emotional and intellectual distance between the character as a younger person and the character at the time of the narration. Many stories and books fulfill the first requirement here but not the second.

- Jane Eyre, for example, looks back on her struggles as a young woman from the perspective of an older woman, fulfilling the first requirement. But Jane doesn't write very critically or objectively about herself as a younger woman—we're encouraged to root for her throughout the book; thus, her narration doesn't fulfill the second requirement.

- One of the best examples of the sort of narrator who fulfills both requirements is Ruth in Marilynne Robinson's novel *Housekeeping*. Much of this book is about how Ruth and her sister, Lucille, two young girls who have either been abandoned or orphaned by all the other adults in their family, end up being looked after by their unconventional aunt, Sylvia.
    - Sylvia makes an attempt to create some stability for her nieces in the family home in Idaho, but she can't resist the pull of a restless life, and in the end, the young Ruth chooses to run off with her aunt while Lucille chooses to stay behind and live a more conventional life. The story is told many years later by the grown-up Ruth, who is now a vastly different person from the young girl she had been.

    - Ruth looks back on her childhood without regret or nostalgia but, instead, with a kind of bemused, mysterious calm that passes no judgment and does not require the reader to make a judgment either.

    - Written in limpid, poetic prose, Ruth's narration takes readers on a spiritual journey that requires us to reconsider everything we may have thought was true about family life, motherhood, and the relations between sisters. Ruth's voice puts us in the mind of an unusual character and shows us the world in a whole new light.

- There are also retrospective first-person narrators who look back on their former selves with disappointment or even contempt, as we saw with David in James Baldwin's novel *Giovanni's Room*. Indeed, we might say that David is an antiheroic narrator: We are expected to take David's story at face value and to endorse his judgment of himself—though in this case, we are meant to share his contempt for himself, rather than endorse his heroism.

The Unreliable Narrator

- The unreliable narrator is one who cannot be trusted by the reader. The simplest version of this narrator simply lies to the reader, revealing his or her deceit at the end of the story. In John Banville's novel *Doctor Copernicus*, there's a section written in the first person by a scholar named Rheticus, who was Copernicus's student but is angry with his teacher. His chapter is full of gossip and criticisms of Copernicus, and only at the end does he confess that a crucial element in his story was invented, casting doubt on nearly everything he has said.

- There are also unreliable narrators who lie to the other characters in the story and often end up deluding themselves. As we saw earlier, the unnamed first-person narrator of Henry James's novella *The Aspern Papers* is a literary critic who is desperate to acquire some old love letters by a long-dead American poet. Throughout the novella, the narrator wrestles with his conscience over what he has done to get the letters, but in the end, he stifles his guilt.

- Another sort of unreliable narrator deludes both himself or herself and the reader. The experience of reading Eudora Welty's story "Why I Live at the P.O." is like being cornered by a talkative and slightly unhinged woman who believes she has been wronged by her family. Because of the narrator's self-pity and her unconscious comic exaggeration, it's clear that her version of events is extremely biased, if not untrue. But unlike Rheticus, who ultimately admits that he has lied to the reader, Welty's narrator sticks to her guns.

- Finally, another variation on the unreliable narrator is the narrator who may or may not be unreliable, but whose truthfulness is never revealed to the reader.
  - One of the most interesting recent examples of such a narrator is in Mohsin Hamid's *The Reluctant Fundamentalist*. The novel is narrated in the first person by a Pakistani man who has attended Princeton and worked on Wall Street, but who, after the events of 9/11, has found himself in reluctant sympathy with the goals of the terrorists.

  - The novel is framed as a long monologue, in which the unnamed narrator tells his life story to an American listener. What makes this narration so unusual is that there are increasing hints that the narrator may be a terrorist and that his listener may be an American intelligence agent sent to kill him. The potential unreliability of the narrator is essential to the final impact of this unsettling and thought-provoking book.

Suggested Reading

Baldwin, *Giovanni's Room*.

Chandler, *The Long Goodbye*.

Fitzgerald, *The Great Gatsby*.

Hamid, *The Reluctant Fundamentalist*.

Melville, *Moby-Dick*.

Robinson, *Housekeeping*.

Twain, *The Adventures of Huckleberry Finn*.

Welty, "Why I Live at the P.O."

1. Try your hand at either the double consciousness that Twain uses in *The Adventures of Huckleberry Finn* or the unreliable narrator technique used by Eurdora Welty or Mohsin Hamid. In the first instance, pick a character whose worldview you disagree with and write in his or her voice, trying to let your own worldview peek through. In the second instance, write from the point of view of a character who is clearly lying about something; try to stay true to the voice while letting the reader know that everything the narrator says is not necessarily true.

He, She, It—Third-Person Point of View
Lecture 17

As mentioned in the last lecture, a first-person narration can be intimate and immediate, but first-person narrators can usually convey only those events that they have witnessed or heard about from another source. The third person, in contrast, has much more range and flexibility. A third-person narration can encompass all sorts of things that a first-person narrator wouldn't know or be able to express. Paradoxically, the third person can also go deeper into an individual character's consciousness than the first person. Perhaps most importantly, the third person is often a more instinctive and natural way to tell a story. In this lecture, we'll look at several varieties of third-person narration and see how they are combined by modern writers.

Close Third Person
- The close third person seems to be the default mode of most contemporary fiction. Here, the writer adopts the point of view of only one character at a time. This narration is similar to the first person because, on the whole, it stays close to what one character knows, thinks, and feels.

- Still, the close third person contains at least the possibility of going deeper into the character's head than a first-person narration does because the third person allows the writer to reveal things about the character's thoughts, feelings, intentions, and prejudices that the character may not know or understand or may not want anybody else to know. In this respect, the close third person can be more comprehensive than the first person, because it allows the writer to show everything about a character, not just what that character chooses to reveal.

- As with other choices in creative writing, using this point of view means that you gain some things and you lose others. With the first person, for example, you can create a unique voice for the character, as Twain does for Huck Finn, and by choosing to tell a story in the close third person, you lose that distinctive voice. In contrast, in the close third person, you can dive as deeply into your characters' minds as Virginia Woolf does in *Mrs. Dalloway*.

- o The moment in *Huckleberry Finn* where Huck decides to help Jim win his freedom—"All right then, I'll *go* to hell"—would not be nearly as thrilling in the close third person because much of the scene's power comes from watching Huck work out the problem for himself.

- o By the same token, the scene in *Mrs. Dalloway* where Clarissa looks into a shop window and her mind skips around with lightning speed would be clumsy in the first person. The intimate but slightly remote view afforded by the close third person allows us to understand Clarissa even better than she understands herself.

- With the close third person, you also can switch from one character to another with relative ease, avoiding the need to reinvent the voice of the narration each time. In other words, you can use the same authorial voice to evoke different characters.

- o The most bravura example of this, of course, is *Mrs. Dalloway*, which often switches point of view within a scene. In most instances, however, writers shift point of view from chapter to chapter. This technique broadens the scope of the story beyond what only one character can know.

- o Alternating points of view in the close third person is a powerful way to tell a long story because it gives you the best of both worlds: Each chapter allows you to inhabit the mind of a single character, but by changing the point of view, you can broaden the scope of the narrative and present different perspectives on the same events. At the most mechanical level, this technique ensures that the reader is present for all the important scenes.

- You can add another dimension to the close third person by including the point-of-view character's first-person thoughts within the third-person narration. A character's thoughts may be indicated by italics or quotation marks, although those treatments may not be appropriate in all cases.

Objective Third Person
- In the objective or remote third person, the narration simply describes what the characters do and say without giving the reader access to their thoughts. At first glance, this narration might seem the same as the recording-eye first person, in which a character who is tangential to the main story relates the events. But there's a crucial difference: With the recording-eye first person, the events are still filtered through a fictional consciousness, who often passes judgment or makes educated guesses as to what the other characters are thinking.
  - Nick Carraway is not central to *The Great Gatsby*, but he views the story of Gatsby and Daisy from a particular point of view— as Daisy's cousin and Gatsby's friend—and his take on the events of the novel colors the reader's understanding.

  - We can compare this with the remote third-person narration in Dashiell Hammett's *The Maltese Falcon*, which watches everything the characters do but doesn't give us direct access to their thoughts and feelings. This kind of third person keeps us at arm's length from its characters, which helps to build suspense but at the cost of a certain iciness.

- The opposite of this remote and noncommittal third person is what we might call the engaged or judgmental third person, in which the narration has a strong opinion about the events it relates, even though that opinion doesn't come from an actual character in the story. This type of third-person narration is commonly found in the novels of the 18th and 19th centuries, when authors often passed judgment on the follies of their characters.
  - This kind of voice works especially well with comic or picaresque novels, such as *Tom Jones*, by the 18th-century English writer Henry Fielding.

o A generation later, we hear a similar voice in Jane Austen, who seems to stand halfway between the warm-blooded, judgmental third person of the 18th century and the cooler but still sympathetic close third person of the 20th century. Much of *Pride and Prejudice* is told in the close third person from Elizabeth Bennet's point of view, but there are also memorable passages in which the author herself passes direct and unmediated judgment.

o Perhaps the most enthusiastically judgmental narrator of all time is Charles Dickens, whose third-person narration often has great fun at the expense of his characters and doesn't shy away from stern moral outrage, especially at the injustices of society.

o Modern writers are no less opinionated than their predecessors, but rather than telling the reader what to think, most contemporary novelists prefer to stand back and let the events of the novel and the actions and ideas of the characters speak for them.

Omniscient Third Person

• The omniscient third person is often described as godlike, but not just because it allows the writer complete access to the created world and the inner lives of the characters. It also allows the writer to give readers the same range of perspectives—from the most all-encompassing views of a community, to the most intimate exchange between two individuals, to a character's most private thoughts.

• There's an overlap here with plotting. As mentioned in an earlier lecture, constructing a plot requires you to choose what to reveal to the reader and when, and when you're writing in this kind of third person, those choices usually depend on which perspective you use.

• The hallmark of the omniscient third person is that you can often swoop in a single chapter—and sometimes in a single passage—from the widest view of the story to the most intimate. A good example of this kind of narrative dexterity is found in chapter 11 of George Eliot's *Middlemarch*.

- o In the first part of the chapter, Eliot tells us, in a straightforward fashion, about a doctor named Lydgate, who is new to the town of Middlemarch, and his interest in marrying a pretty young woman named Rosamond Vincy. Eliot bluntly states that Lydgate is "young, poor, and ambitious" and that the chief quality he wants in a wife is beauty and charm. Eliot also lets us know that Rosamond is interested in Lydgate, too, because she considers herself too good for the boring young men she grew up with.

- o Along the way in this passage of pure exposition, Eliot masterfully fits Lydgate and Rosamond within the social hierarchy of the town, while also discussing the fact that love and marriage can disarrange that social hierarchy. It is, in other words, as godlike a perspective as possible, mostly cool, even-handed, and remote, with a few flashes of authorial judgment.

- o Then, Eliot narrows her focus to the breakfast table of the Vincy household, where Rosamond, her brother Fred, and their mother discuss a wide variety of topics. Here, Eliot vividly evokes the individual characters and their relationships, while taking care of an important moment in the plot and giving the reader information that will be important later on. And it's all done in a third-person point of view that is halfway between a recording eye and a judgmental authorial voice.

- It's important to note that an omniscient third-person narration can also incorporate the close third person. In *Anna Karenina*, Tolstoy writes much of the novel in the same omniscient third person that Eliot uses, keeping us at a slight remove from the characters. But he also delves into a modern-seeming close third person, especially with Anna herself.

Combining Points of View

- Although it may be true that the close third person remains the default mode for many writers, you'll also find that most writers feel free to mix and match the varieties of the third person in surprising and innovative ways.

- Much of the narration of the American detective novelist George Pelecanos, for instance, is of the recording-eye variety, with detailed descriptions in spare language of what his characters look like, what they wear, and what they say and do. But occasionally, his narration varies from the remote third person to the close third person. Interestingly, Pelecanos also occasionally allows himself to step in and pass judgment on his characters.

- Such judgments help make it clear that an author doesn't necessarily endorse everything his or her protagonist does. You can do this in the first person only by implication, but in the third person, you can come right out and say what you think.

Suggested Reading

Austen, *Pride and Prejudice*.

Dickens, *Bleak House*.

Eliot, *Middlemarch*.

Hammett, *The Maltese Falcon*.

Hynes, *The Wild Colonial Boy*.

Martin, *A Song of Ice and Fire*.

Pelecanos, *The Cut*.

1. Pick a stressful or contentious situation between two characters—an argument between a husband and wife, for example, or an interrogation scene in which a detective is trying to get a confession out of a suspect. Then, tell the scene three ways: once in the close third person from the point of view of one character, such as the detective; once in the close third person from the point of view of the other character; and once in the omniscient third person, showing the same situation from a godlike perspective.

Evoking Setting and Place in Fiction
Lecture 18

E very story has a setting, but setting is not equally important to all stories. For some narratives, setting is a sort of painted theatrical backdrop against which the story plays out, and that backdrop can be changed for another one without fundamentally changing the story itself. In most contemporary fiction, however, setting is important, and much of what makes a novel or story memorable is the author's careful evocation of a particular place and time. In this lecture, we'll talk about some of the purposes to which setting can be put in a narrative and some of the ways in which setting can be evoked.

Setting as a Metaphor
- In many narratives, setting can be a metaphor for the narrative as a whole. One of the most famous examples here is the opening paragraph of *Bleak House*, Charles Dickens's novel about a complicated and never-ending lawsuit in mid-19th-century England.
  - Before we meet a single character in *Bleak House* and before the plot even starts, Dickens indelibly evokes a vision of dark, dirty London, full of filthy animals, ill-tempered pedestrians, and people wheezing and shivering in the all-encompassing fog.

  - This exceptionally vivid evocation of setting serves two purposes: It vividly evokes the sensory details of London in the mind of the reader—the darkness, the cold, the dirt—and it makes the setting serve as a metaphor for the misty, insinuating, impenetrably foggy coils of the lawsuit itself.

- In J. G. Farrell's historical novel *Troubles*, which is about the Irish rebellion against British rule in the years after World War I, the main setting is a giant resort hotel on the Irish coast called the Majestic, and it serves throughout the novel as a metaphor for the grand, ornate, and crumbling edifice of the British Empire.

- At the end of the novel, the Irish Republican Army burns the hotel to the ground, not only destroying the hotel but metaphorically destroying the dominance of the Protestants and British in Ireland. On the last page, a gentle and befuddled retired British army major surveys the ruins, including the skeletons of the hundreds of cats that lived in the hotel.

- Even readers who don't know anything about the history of the Irish Revolution understand that the major is surveying the ruins of an empire, not just a burned-down hotel.

- Note that the descriptions of foggy, dirty London in *Bleak House* and the Majestic Hotel in *Troubles* are also full of vivid sensory details that draw readers into the scene, putting them in the moment even if they don't consciously pick up on the metaphor. Even when a setting is used for a metaphorical purpose, it should be visceral and vivid, allowing us to experience that imaginary world as if we were characters in the story.

Setting to Evoke Mood
- Setting can also be used to evoke mood, especially when the point is to evoke a strong vicarious emotion, such as the feeling of fear readers get from a horror story or the feeling of suspense they get from a thriller.

- Consider part of the description of a haunted house from the early pages of Judith Hawkes's marvelously creepy novel *Julian's House*:

> Inside the gate a silence falls. Leaves stir and are still. At the foot of the porch steps the silence deepens, wrapped around with the fragrance of the shallow pink roses that twine the uprights and shadow the wide boards with their leaves. And yet it is more than a silence, as the leaves stir and again are still: it is a silence of breath held, of a sob stifled in a pillow, the silence that follows the blow of a fist upon a table. In the moving leaves this silence seems to murmur in its sleep—of too many closed doors, keys turning smoothly in well-oiled locks, glances exchanged without words. (p. 12)

- Even if we hadn't already been told that this is a haunted house, it would be impossible for anybody to read this description and not understand immediately that there is something wrong with this house—that there is something bad waiting inside.

- Notice that Hawkes uses the word *silence* six times in this description. Although normally the repetition of a word that many times in so short a passage would be anathema to writers, here, it has the effect of making the silence ominous. Note, too, that *silence* is paired with active verbs— *falls*, *deepens*, *murmur*[*s*]—changing it from an absence of sound to an active presence in the house.

Setting to Evoke Character

- In addition, setting can be used to tell readers about the characters in a story. For example, a description of a room or a house is often used to tell us something about the person who lives there.

- One of the major plotlines in George Eliot's *Middlemarch* is the ill-advised marriage between Dorothea Brooke, an intense young woman in her early 20s, and Edward Casaubon, a dry and humorless scholar who is 30 years her senior. Early in the book, after their surprise engagement, Dorothea goes to visit Mr. Casaubon's home:

   > The building, of greenish stone, was in the old English style, not ugly, but small-windowed and melancholy-looking …. In this latter end of autumn … the house too had an air of autumnal decline, and Mr. Casaubon, when he presented himself, had no bloom that could be thrown into relief by that background. (pp. 73–74)

- Nearly everything that Eliot says about the house—that it is "not ugly, but small-windowed and melancholy" and that it has an air of "autumnal decline"—could also be said about Casaubon himself. The last clause of the passage is one of the great backhanded insults in English literature: the fact that there is nothing about Casaubon himself that could be "thrown into relief" by his joyless home.

Setting to Evoke Time and Movement

- Setting can also be used to evoke the passage of time and the movement of characters through a landscape. Tolkien is especially skillful at evoking the geography of Middle Earth—in part, simply because he delights in evoking the natural world but also because these passages literally slow the narrative down, which has the effect of evoking the slow passage of the characters, moving on foot through a vast and often spectacular landscape.

  In a chase scene, Rosemary Sutcliff skillfully evokes both motion and the landscape of the Scottish highlands with such phrases as "skirting a reed-fringed upland pool" and "swerving from a patch of bog."

  - A passage in *The Two Towers* in which Frodo and Sam pass through the land of Ithilien evokes both the vastness of the landscape through which they are moving and their own sense of wonder at it. The fact that the reader is required to slow down during this passage and to literally stop and smell the flowers also evokes the slowness of their journey.

  - Among other techniques, the passage effectively shifts focus from the long distance to the close-up: We first see the mountains as "a long curve that was lost in the distance," but in the next sentence, we get particular types of trees—"fir and cedar and cypress." Finally, we see individual harbingers of spring: fronds piercing moss, green-fingered larches, and flowers opening in the turf.

- Of course, setting doesn't have to slow down the narrative; it can also evoke speed and danger. In a chase scene from Rosemary Sutcliff's *The Eagle of the Ninth*, we delight in the vivid evocation of the landscape in its own right—luminous green bogs, bronze tides of dying heather—but we also note that Sutcliff skillfully interweaves flashes of landscape description with breathless action.

A Continuum of Setting

- The many ways in which setting can be evoked fall between two ends of a continuum: At one end, setting is evoked by stopping the narrative in its tracks and describing a place or a time period. At the other end, setting is evoked only minimally.

  ○ In general—though not always—the first method is used in narratives similar to *Bleak House* or *Troubles*, where the setting is important to the story, while at the other extreme, when the setting isn't that important, writers don't bother with it as much.

  ○ In between, there are many variations, including evoking setting as you go, inserting a few telling details along the way without stopping the action. As always, most novels and short stories fall somewhere in between, combining the various methods.

- In narratives that include standalone descriptions of setting, how the writer uses them depends on the point of view of the novel, whether it's the omniscient third person, limited third person, or first person.

  ○ The omniscient third person is almost cinematic. The opening of *Bleak House*, for example, is like a crane shot in a movie, starting high up—"smoke lowering down from chimney-pots, making a soft black drizzle"—and slowly descending to street level—"dogs, undistinguishable in mire." This passage gives the mind's eye something to look at, and it introduces a central metaphor for the plot.

- When a standalone description of setting is told from the limited third-person or first-person point of view, it also evokes character. How the character sees the setting—what details he or she picks out as important—tells us something about the person through whose eyes we, the readers, are seeing them.

- When setting is described from the first-person point of view, it can become even more multilayered. For example, setting is important to the novels of Raymond Chandler, but it's also important that the setting is seen through the eyes and mind of Chandler's protagonist, the private detective Philip Marlowe. Marlowe's descriptions tell us a great deal about himself.

• Writers who only scarcely evoke setting often use a kind of shorthand, relying on the fact that certain places, street names, or even brand names are familiar to the reader and will be evocative of time and place. The crime thrillers of George Pelecanos, for example, are specifically set in Washington, DC, and Pelecanos skillfully mixes real street and place names in Washington with brief bits of description.

• Whether you choose to lavish your reader with a richly detailed description or simply say that your detective walked into a Starbucks, remember that in most cases, how you use setting depends on the overall purpose of your narrative. Scene by scene, you want to lavish detailed descriptions on settings that recur or are especially important, but you need only a line or two to evoke settings that don't matter quite as much or that appear only once.

Suggested Reading

Austen, *Pride and Prejudice*.

Chandler, *The Big Sleep*.

Dickens, *Bleak House*.

Eliot, *Middlemarch*.

Farrell, *Troubles*.

Hawkes, *Julian's House*.

Pelecanos, *The Cut*.

Sutcliff, *The Eagle of the Ninth*.

Tolkien, *The Two Towers*.

Writing Exercises

1. Try describing the same setting from the point of view of two different characters who want different things. For example, consider Sarah and Brad, the unhappily married couple in our narrative from the first lecture. As you may recall, they're at a baseball game; try to describe the ballpark from Sarah's point of view, bearing in mind that she's about to ask for a divorce, and then from Brad's, bearing in mind that he has no idea what she's about to ask him.

2. You might also explore the importance of a particular setting to a narrative by setting a scene from a famous novel or story in a radically different place or time from the original version. Can you rewrite a scene from, say, *The Adventures of Huckleberry Finn* that is set someplace other than the Mississippi? Could one of the scenes from *The Great Gatsby* take place at any other place or time than Long Island in the Jazz Age?

Pacing in Scenes and Narratives
Lecture 19

Every narrative has a tempo. Some stories are fast-paced and breathless, some are slow and meditative, and as always, there's a vast middle ground of narratives where the tempo varies throughout the work, depending on what the writer is trying to evoke at a particular moment. In fiction, this tempo is called *pacing*—a rather slippery concept because it's so subjective. Some readers crave constant action and clever plot twists, while others want a story that lingers over the intimate details of a character's sensibility and relationships. Given that no book can be all things to all readers, the trick for the writer becomes finding the right tempo, or variety of tempos, for his or her particular story.

Introduction to Pacing
- Pacing in fiction encompasses two levels: the pace of the narrative as a whole and the pace of individual chapters and scenes. Both of these ways of looking at pacing are based on a sort of proportion or balance. Indeed, the essence of pacing is a kind of juggling act, by which writers gauge how much information they want to get across, how many words or pages they have to do it in, and how much patience they hope the reader has.

- One feature of pacing a writer must address is the length of time a story or scene takes in the world of the narrative versus the time it takes for someone to read it. On the whole, a long book that depicts a short period of time will probably be slower paced than a short book or a short story that depicts a long period of time.

- But length itself is not a reliable measure of the pace of a narrative. You also have to consider the balance between the length of the story and the number of incidents and characters within it. We might call this the *density* of the narrative.

- A third kind of balance to consider is that between action and exposition or between scene and summary.
    - In most narratives, the writer shifts back and forth between modes of storytelling. On the one hand, writers usually dramatize the most important and interesting events as separate scenes, with the full complement of action, dialogue, and setting. On the other hand, writers often need to get across a good deal of important background or expository information that isn't necessarily very dramatic.

    - Expository passages often stand outside the time sequence of the narrative—such as when you pause the action to describe a setting or to tell a character's backstory—or you might simply summarize a long period of time in a few paragraphs in order to get the characters quickly from one place to another or from one dramatic moment in the story to the next.

Pacing a Whole Narrative

- Leo Tolstoy's *The Death of Ivan Ilyich* opens with a short chapter in which a group of Ivan Ilyich's fellow lawyers talk about his recent death. After that, Tolstoy spends the next 11 pages or so of this 50-page narrative summarizing the events of the first 44 years of Ivan's life. The son of a civil servant, he becomes a civil servant himself, and his professional life is devoted to rising through the bureaucracy, while his personal life is devoted to social climbing, marriage, and fatherhood.
    - The overall effect of the story depends on Tolstoy convincing us of Ivan's ordinariness, but because the first 44 years of his life are the least dramatic part of the story, Tolstoy summarizes them at a rapid clip. He tells us what we need to know—and no more—as quickly and efficiently as possible.

    - About halfway through the novella, Ivan falls off a ladder, and his injury leads to a mysterious illness that ends up killing him only three months later. Suddenly, this Everyman's life has become dramatic, and having raced through the first 44 years of his life in 11 pages, Tolstoy spreads his last three months out over 35 pages. The pace slows, and there's a greater amount of detail and a sharper focus on his day-to-day moments as Ivan weakens. As the story reaches Ivan's last day, it slows down even more, devoting the last page and a half to the final hour of his life.

o Except for the opening chapter, *The Death of Ivan Ilyich* starts out as fast-paced exposition and becomes slower and more dramatic as it goes on, until the end, where it lingers over the very last moment in Ivan Ilyich's life.

• Let's compare this story with Alice Munro's "The Beggar Maid." This story goes for 33 pages, the first 30 of which depict the first year of the relationship between its two main characters, Patrick and Rose.

o Instead of segregating the exposition and putting it all at once at the beginning, the way Tolstoy does, Munro shifts effortlessly back and forth between vividly dramatized moments and sharp passages of exposition.

o At the center of the story is a fully dramatized scene in which Rose breaks up with Patrick, which is then followed by a more expository scene in which she changes her mind. Then, in the last three pages of the story, Munro

The nature of Alice Munro's "The Beggar Maid" dictates the story's pacing, starting slow and speeding up to lead us to the devastating scene at the airport in the end.

summarizes Rose and Patrick's unhappy 10-year marriage in five paragraphs before giving us a final scene 9 years after their divorce: They see each other in the airport in Toronto, and Rose is shocked when Patrick makes a hateful face at her, a "timed explosion of disgust and loathing."

- The pacing and the balance between action and exposition of each of these stories reflect the different intents of their authors.

    o Tolstoy wants to show us that most of Ivan Ilyich's life has been shallow and selfish; thus, he races through the first 44 years in order to linger on the last three months, when Ivan's suffering allows him to feel compassion for his wife and son in his last moments. In order to do this, the novella needs to start at a rapid pace and slow down as it goes, reflecting Ivan's own moral and spiritual journey.

    o In "The Beggar Maid," however, Munro is more like a lawyer building a case. To prepare for that focused moment of loathing on the last page, she needs to show in slow, patient, dramatic detail why Patrick and Rose should never have married in the first place and why they did anyway. Having done that, she can then fast-forward through the marriage itself and through the 9 years after it before dramatizing the final encounter.

- Eleanor Catton's *The Luminaries* is set during a gold rush on the west coast of New Zealand during the 1860s, and it has a complicated plot involving secrets, conspiracies, and betrayals. Interestingly, Catton chooses not to dramatize many of the most striking scenes—including a shipwreck and a possible murder—and, instead, structures the novel as a series of long conversations between various combinations of her large and diverse cast of characters.

    o During these conversations, the buried plot of the novel is slowly revealed. There are a few passages of scene setting and action, and in nearly every chapter, Catton pauses the conversation to tell us something about the history or psychology of one or more of the characters in it. But on the whole, the novel moves at a steady and unvarying pace, as the reader eavesdrops on these conversations in real time.

- o In the end, the novel is more about the nature of storytelling itself—about how people construct reality out of the stories they tell each other—than it is about the working out of the actual mystery.

- Written by a veteran of World War I under the shadow of World War II, *The Lord of the Rings* is a narrative about the end of one world and the dawn of a new one and the effect of the cataclysm on both individuals and whole races of people.
  - o Because he wishes to immerse us in this epic tale, Tolkien varies the pace throughout the book, letting us know what's important and what's mere background or scene setting by slowing down and dramatizing the most important moments and summarizing the less important ones.

  - o Unlike Catton, whose intent is more postmodern and cerebral, Tolkien's intent is to allow the reader to visit Middle Earth and participate in its history. Thus, he skillfully varies the pace, alternating thrilling or dramatic scenes with passages of exposition or backstory, partly to give the reader a breather and partly to prepare us for what comes next.

Pacing Individual Scenes

- How a scene is paced depends partly on its function in the narrative as a whole and partly on the author's intent: Is it important or not? Is it inherently dramatic or not?

- Scenes that introduce new characters to a narrative tend to be played out at a slow pace, in real time. This is also true of scenes of domestic life that are intended to show the characters at home, in a setting that is familiar to them.

- In contrast, intensely dramatic or violent scenes can be played out either fast or slow, depending on your intent. At the end of Melville's *Moby-Dick*, for example, Captain Ahab and the crew of the whaling ship *Pequod* chase the great white whale for three days, and the suspense is stretched out for 40 pages. But then, Ahab's death happens in a flash. The effect is shocking and ruthless—a dazzling example of how a sudden shift in pacing can open the abyss at the reader's feet.

- Slowing the pace of a scene can allow you to wring the last bit of suspense or mystery out of it. In John le Carré's *Tinker, Tailor, Soldier, Spy*, the aging spy George Smiley has been assigned to discover the identity of a Soviet double-agent, who has been working at the highest level of British intelligence for 30 years.
  - The book's pace varies throughout, but in its climactic scene, Smiley is hiding with a gun in the kitchen of a safe house, where he has lured the double-agent. He knows that the next voice he hears will tell him which of his trusted friends and colleagues is a traitor. At this point, le Carré slows the narrative down, telling us every detail, making us sweat alongside Smiley.

  - The events in this passage—an unseen man coming to the door and Smiley's racing thoughts—would take only a few seconds in real life, but le Carré almost cruelly slows them down, making us wait for the big reveal.

Suggested Reading

Burroway, *Writing Fiction*.

Catton, *The Luminaries*.

Eliot, *Middlemarch*.

Le Carré, *Tinker, Tailor, Soldier, Spy*.

Melville, *Moby-Dick*.

Munro, "The Beggar Maid."

Pelecanos, *The Cut*.

Tolkien, *The Lord of the Rings*.

Tolstoy, *The Death of Ivan Ilyich*.

Writing Exercise

1. Select one incident from something you've written and try writing it several different ways—as a summary, as a close third-person narrative, or as a long dialogue scene; take note of how the difference in pace and approach changes the effect. Then compare the results and see which one best serves the intent of the narrative you've written.

Building Scenes
Lecture 20

W riters approach the day-to-day process of composition in many ways, and of course, what you do as a writer each day depends on the overall shape of your narrative and on the purpose of the particular passage you're working on. Writers also differ on what they consider the fundamentals of writing fiction: the plot, character development, ideas to be conveyed, the crafting of elegant sentences, and so on. In the end, no matter how you approach the day-to-day process, every writer is faced with the prospect of making the whole thing hang together. We'll talk about that in our next two lectures, but in this lecture, we'll discuss what a writer does each day, that is, creating individual scenes.

Defining *Scenes*

- In his book *The Art of Fiction*, John Gardner defines a scene as everything "that is included in an unbroken flow of action from one incident in time to another." For Gardner, this unbroken flow can include movement through space from one place to another, as long as there isn't a big jump in time. In other words, a scene shows more or less everything that happens to a character, or between two or more characters, during a particular, discrete span of time, without any interruptions in the flow of that time, except for flashbacks or brief passages of exposition.

- There are, of course, many types of scenes, ranging from brief scenes featuring only a few characters in a narrowly defined setting to epic scenes that show many characters in a vast setting. There are scenes that are merely transitional, scenes that are pivotal moments in the plot, scenes where we learn the thoughts of only a single character, scenes in which the only action is conversation among the characters, and scenes full of violent, thrilling action.

- Deciding what you make into a scene as opposed to what you choose to reveal through exposition—in other words, what you choose to dramatize rather than summarize—is generally fairly easy. You usually want to dramatize the most important or interesting parts of the story, while relying on exposition to get across essential but less interesting information.

Requirements of Scenes

- An individual scene must meet at least two requirements at the same time: It must advance the larger narrative, or at least fit into it, and it must be interesting in its own right. In other words, a writer needs to balance the scene's position in the whole story with its own inherent drama. The way to achieve this balance is to remember that a scene should be no longer than it needs to be for its purpose within the story as a whole.

- These two balanced requirements—the intent of the narrative and the inherent interest of the scene—can vary enormously from one narrative to another.
    - George Pelecanos's hard-boiled detective novel *The Cut* is a fast-paced narrative, written with efficiency and economy. Its young detective, Spero Lucas, occasionally takes time out from the case he's working on to have an erotic interlude with a young woman. Such scenes move at the same brisk pace as the rest of the book, and they serve to tell us something we wouldn't otherwise know about Spero, but because they aren't central to the story, they tend to be much shorter and more expository than the scenes that advance Spero's investigations.

    - In a more expansive narrative, such as *Ulysses* or *Moby-Dick*, a scene can go on for pages simply because the author thinks it is inherently interesting. Melville, for example, devotes long passages or even whole chapters to describing the work of a whaling vessel, the natural history of whales, and other topics. These scenes advance the overall purpose of the book, which is to evoke a way of life in as much detail as possible, but they aren't necessarily concerned with advancing the plot.

    - And with some books, the point of the novel isn't the plot at all but the individual scenes that make up the plot. Even though

The Lecturer's Tale has a plot, the true purpose of the book is to make fun of the excesses of modern literary theory. For this reason, the book is basically a series of satirical set pieces. These set pieces aren't entirely self-contained—each pushes the plot a little further along—but each chapter or scene is mainly intended to be amusing for its own sake.

- Again, how long a scene goes on and whether it should be included at all depends on the intent of the narrative as a whole.

  o A crime novel, such as *The Cut*, needs to move quickly; if it slows down, it dies. Trying to squeeze in a long chapter about the history of detective work would throw off the whole story.

© Comstock Images/Stockbyte/Thinkstock.

The Lecturer's Tale satirizes academics who put literary criticism above actual works of art; its scenes are more focused on amusing the reader than advancing the plot.

  o *The Lecturer's Tale*, however, has a different metabolism. The reader is not meant to race through it but to enjoy each scene as it comes. The scenes in each book have a different pace and structure because the intent of each book is different.

Scene Transitions

- Transitioning into and out of scenes can vex even experienced writers. Such transitions can vary enormously, depending on the intent of the scene, its length, its importance in the narrative, and so on.

- Scenes that take place early in the narrative need more setup, on the whole, than scenes that appear later. When you're introducing characters, situations, or settings for the first time, you need to spend more time describing them than you do later on, when the reader already knows who the character is or what the setting looks like. You can often take your time in these early scenes, describing the setting and characters in some detail and letting the characters talk a bit more digressively than they might in later scenes.

- Short scenes tend to need less introduction than longer, more dramatic scenes. You can signal the start of a new scene with something as simple as a space break in the text or, if time has passed since the last section, with a simple phrase, such as "The next day ..." or "A few hours later ...." Scenes that are longer, more important, or more dramatic require more buildup at the start.

  o For example, in "The Beggar Maid," Alice Munro begins the scene in which Rose breaks up with Patrick with a brief description of Rose's walk from her room to Patrick's apartment. This description slows down the narrative and lets us know that something important is about to happen, providing a bumper between the fast-paced mix of exposition and miniature scenes that came immediately before it and the slower and more dramatic scene that's about to start.

  o Munro then ends the scene abruptly and dramatically, befitting the emotionally turbulent nature of the encounter, as Rose storms out of Patrick's apartment: "'I don't want to see you, ever!' she said viciously. But at the door she turned and said in a normal and regretful voice, 'Good-bye.'" (p. 96)

- Another way to transition into a scene is to begin it *in medias res*. The chief advantage of this approach is that it adds energy and urgency to the narrative. It also engages readers on a deeper level, forcing them to pay attention to what's going on.

  o For example, the opening sequence of Eleanor Catton's epic historical mystery *The Luminaries* introduces a character named Walter Moody, who has just arrived at a remote gold rush community on the west coast of New Zealand in 1866. In the opening pages, he finds himself in a hotel lounge with 12 other men, who tell him a long, complicated story about a suspicious death, a suicide attempt, and a fortune in gold, all of which happened two weeks before Moody even arrived.

- o Catton runs the risk here that the reader might feel overwhelmed, rather like Moody himself does, walking into a group of people he's never met before who are talking about something complicated that happened before he arrived. But she constructs this opening scene so expertly, with such attention to the detail, that she hooks the reader into a mystery that isn't fully explained until 800 pages later.

- Transitioning out of a scene is perhaps a little less difficult than transitioning into one. Once the main purpose of the scene has played out—the new character has been sufficiently introduced or the plot point has been made—you generally want to wrap it up as quickly as possible. For some kinds of narrative, you might want to end with a sort of punchline—a witticism from a character or a sudden revelation—but even with narratives that aren't driven by plot, you don't want to linger over the scene after its purpose has been fulfilled.

- There can also be transitions within a scene, such as when a writer pauses to provide some exposition or segue into a flashback.
  - o Again, *The Luminaries* is made up mostly of long, dramatized scenes, but because the plot is so complicated, Catton often pauses the action to introduce an extended flashback or some exposition about a character's history or psychology.

  - o Because the novel is written in the style of a 19th-century novel, sometimes Catton directly addresses the reader in a manner that calls attention to the transition itself. At other times, she slips effortlessly from drama to exposition with hardly any transition at all.

- Transitioning into and out of flashbacks is generally fairly straightforward. If it's a short flashback, you might signal the shift by putting the whole episode in italics. If the flashback is from the point of view of a particular character, you can simply write something like, "Leo thought back to the conversation he'd had with Anna the day before." A more subtle way to signal a flashback is with a change in verb tense—from the present tense to the past or the simple past to the past perfect.

Stories within Stories

- Although some scenes are just small bursts of drama that can be truncated or incomplete, most of the weight in a narrative is carried by fully dramatized scenes with a beginning, middle, and end. These major scenes are basically small stories within the larger story.

- Even if a major scene couldn't stand alone outside the context of the whole narrative, it should have the structure of a simple story. Earlier, we discussed fractals, the mathematical concept of a pattern that repeats itself at every level of magnification. It's not true that each individual scene should reproduce the structure or plot of the larger narrative, but it helps to remember that any story made of scenes is basically made of smaller stories.

Suggested Reading

Catton, *The Luminaries*.

Gardner, *The Art of Fiction*.

Hynes, *The Lecturer's Tale*.

———, *Next*.

———, *The Wild Colonial Boy*.

Munro, "The Beggar Maid."

1. Choose an undramatized moment from a story of your own or from a story or novel you admire and turn it into a full-fledged dramatic scene. In other words, take a moment from a story that is only alluded to or is depicted only briefly in an expository passage and dramatize it fully. For example, you might dramatize the moment that Hamlet is told that his father has died, a scene that doesn't appear in Shakespeare's play. Use as many words or pages as you need and turn that scene into a little story, with a beginning, middle, and end, making sure that the scene you write contributes to the larger narrative. This exercise will give you practice in making a scene self-contained, as well as making it an integral part of the larger story.

Should I Write in Drafts?
Lecture 21

From day to day, most writers focus on the individual elements that go into the writing of fiction: characters, dialogue, plot, setting, and so on. But sooner or later, you will have a completed draft, and you'll have to start worrying about whether or not the whole thing works. In this lecture and the next one, we'll talk about working with the narrative as a whole. The next lecture covers the process of revision, but as we'll discover, that process is closely linked with the process of composition. In this lecture, then, we'll talk about composing drafts. We'll begin with the pros and cons of writing the whole narrative out from beginning to end before you start changing it.

First Drafts
- Every completed writing project has at least a first draft. For some writers, that first draft is also the final draft, but most of the time, writers don't intend the first draft to be the finished work of art. In fact, it's not even supposed to be very good.

- The fact that first drafts are notoriously bad is not just an unfortunate byproduct of the creative process; it's a necessity. Think of writing a first draft as mining for gold the way it was done in such films as *The Treasure of the Sierra Madre*. Imagine yourself squatting awkwardly in a stream, sifting through dirt by hand to get a few flakes of gold. Expecting your first draft to be perfect is about as likely as the possibility that you will pick nuggets straight out of the dirt with your fingers.

- It's also true, however, that the experience of writing a first draft can be thrilling, and it's often more fun than the more grueling and painstaking work of revision. In many cases, writing a first draft is your only opportunity to experience the story in the way the reader will; that is, it's the only chance you'll have to find your way through the story scene by scene, without necessarily knowing what comes next or how it turns out.

It's the only time in the creative process when you can fully experience the thrill of discovery.

- o Obviously, if you've created a detailed outline of your narrative or you know how it will end, you won't be experiencing it in complete ignorance of what comes next, the way a reader would.

- o But even if you think you know where the story is going, you're likely to encounter any number of fruitful surprises while writing the first draft—surprises that will deepen or complicate the outline you worked out in advance. These surprises may lead you to change the outline or even throw it away. They may also lead you to change the ending.

- o Even if you're working from an outline or think you know what your final destination is, during the early days of composition, you are an explorer moving through territory that no one else has ever crossed before.

- Writing a first draft can also be fun because a first draft is not supposed to be economical.

- o You will probably find it fruitful to make your first draft the longest draft, putting in everything you can think of, then putting in some more. Especially at the beginning of a project, you're likely to be bursting with ideas and possibilities, and it's in your best interest to put as many of them down on paper as you can, without worrying too much about plausibility, consistency, or logic.

- o You don't have to worry about whether your first draft will be interesting, because chances are that no one will ever see it except yourself and a few trusted readers.

- o The reason for writing a long first draft is twofold: (1) The more material you put into it, the more material you have to work with later on, and (2) as we've said, writing a first draft is a process of exploration. You won't know for certain what the story is or who the characters are until you have the whole thing in front of you. The experience of writing everything down can change what you thought you were doing in profound ways.

- Another good practice is to write your first draft as quickly as possible. The time for the careful calibration of phrases, sentences, and paragraphs comes later. To begin with, you don't want to worry too much about pacing, about what works and what doesn't, or even about consistency. Keep in mind the motto of the songwriter and performer Nick Lowe: "Bash it out now and tart it up later."

  o Not only will speed help you get as many ideas on the page as you can, some of that energy may well survive into the finished work.

  o In an interview in *The New York Times*, the mystery writer Michael Connelly talked about his technique for writing fiction: "I have always felt that the books I have written fastest have been my best—because I caught an unstoppable momentum in the writing."

- The suggestion that you write a long first draft quickly can apply to any writer, at every level of experience, but it may be especially true for writers who are just starting out, especially for first novelists. Creative writing courses can be helpful, but in the end, you learn how to write a book by writing one. You learn by trial and error, and you give yourself the most scope for that process to be fruitful if you write an expansive, baggy, inconsistent, very likely unpublishable, and maybe even unreadable first draft.

Evolution of the Writing Process
- During the heyday of the novel in the 19th century, it was probably uncommon for a writer to compose several complete drafts of a novel before publishing it because many novels at the time were published as serials. These sections of novels appeared in weekly or monthly installments in newspapers or magazines over the course of a year or two.

  o Charles Dickens is especially famous for having written his novels in installments, sometimes working only two weeks ahead of publication. He started writing *David Copperfield*, for example, in February 1849, and the first installment was published only three months later. He didn't complete the book until November of 1850, so that the public had already started reading the novel long before he finished writing it.

o This means that Dickens never did more than one complete draft of *David Copperfield*, and it means that he must have thought the novel through in great detail before he started writing.

o Dickens may have done drafts of individual chapters or sections; he certainly rewrote things as he went along; and it's entirely possible that he may have changed his mind about the later chapters that he had outlined but hadn't written yet. But Dickens didn't have the option of making changes to the chapters that had already been published.

o That may have handicapped him as far as plotting went, but even so, much of Dickens's work has an irresistible narrative momentum that is partly a reflection of his own boundless energy and partly a product of how he wrote the books—on deadline, a chapter at a time, just two weeks ahead of the printer.

• The commercial realities of publishing serial fiction in the 19th century affected the daily creative process of writers, dictating that books be written on the fly, without repeated drafts. In our own time, changes in technology have also caused changes in the way writers compose a whole narrative.

Writing by hand is more time consuming than typing on a computer, but it can be a fruitful way to make yourself slow down and think about what you're trying to accomplish.

o Many writers who once wrote

multiple drafts out in longhand now write only one complete draft of their work on the computer, making as many changes as they need to during the writing process.

o   In other words, although each individual chapter may go through multiple drafts, many writers no longer compose one complete draft of a whole book; they don't advance to the next chapter until the current one is more or less finished.

One Draft versus Multiple Drafts

- If you've thought about a book for a long time, when you sit down to actually write it, you may find that you spend the most amount of time on the first three or four chapters. Once you have a firm foundation for the characters, the plot, and the setting, the later chapters may come easier.

- The creative process may also become easier for you as you gain experience as a writer. When you're writing your first story or novel, you're learning as you go, but as you become more experienced, you no longer have to teach yourself how to write dialogue, build suspense, and so on.

- Of course, there is always more than one way of doing things. No doubt, there are many experienced writers who continue to write in multiple complete drafts throughout their careers, and no doubt there are some rare novices who dash out a masterpiece in a first draft. As always, you should do what works best for you.

- In the end, whether you write multiple drafts or only one depends on the nature of the project. A plot-driven story that takes place in chronological order may be easier to write in one draft than a story that encompasses flashbacks or other nonchronological events.

- Note, too, that as you gain experience, you may no longer follow the advice to write long first drafts. You might find that your early drafts of individual scenes—not to mention the finished manuscript—are shorter than later drafts. In other words, you may become an "accretive" writer:

With each subsequent draft, you gather a little more material and go back to earlier scenes to fill in more details.

Suggested Reading

Ackroyd, *Dickens*.

Lamott, *Bird by Bird*.

Writing Exercise

1. Try some of the different writing techniques mentioned in this lecture with one of your own scenes or chapters. For those who are more accustomed to using a computer, try drafting a scene in longhand to make yourself slow down and think as you write. You might also think about how you usually compose a scene or chapter, then try the opposite technique. In other words, if you're the sort of writer who dashes through a scene without looking back, try slowing down and revising as you go, writing your first paragraph multiple times until you think it's perfect before proceeding to the next one. If you're already the sort of writer who revises as you go, try typing out a scene as fast and furiously as possible, without stopping and looking back. With either approach, you may hate the result—in which case, you can go back to your old way of doing things—or you might find that sometimes, for certain purposes, changing your process can lead to interesting results.

Revision without Tears
Lecture 22

In the early stages of composing a work of fiction, you're often caught up in the thrill of discovery, creating unique situations and characters. Whatever frustrations you may experience in the act of creation are offset by the sheer pleasure of making something new. But then, having created a beautiful, imaginative draft, you have to sit down and look for everything you did wrong. Revision is about confronting your own mistakes and fixing them in such a way that the reader never knows there were any mistakes to begin with. It can be hard and unpleasant work, but in this lecture, we'll look at strategies for revision that can make it less intimidating.

The Daunting Task of Revision

- Much of what makes revision difficult is that you have to consider your draft on every level, more or less all at once. It's the one time in the whole process where you cannot avoid having to think about everything. You have to ask yourself not only if the entire narrative works as a whole, but if all its individual parts do what they're supposed to do and whether they all pull in the same direction. Is each character complete and believable? Are the point of view, verb tense, and setting appropriate? Does each chapter and scene round off and lead to the next? Are your sentences interesting, elegant, and memorable?

- One way to make this daunting task less intimidating is to prepare for revision from the very start. The motto "Bash it out now and tart it up later" is a reminder to forge ahead energetically, but it also serves to underscore the idea that getting the story down on paper is only the beginning of the process; you will have to "tart it up"—change things—later on.

- Composing and revising are inextricably linked, and how you revise depends in large part on how you composed the draft in the first place.

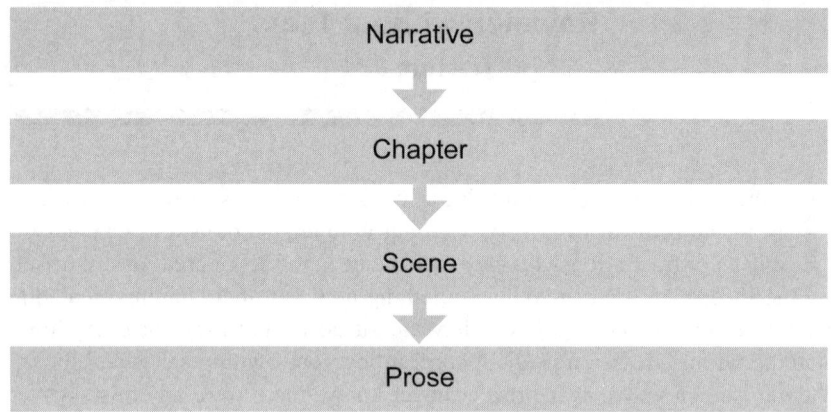

When revising, you need to think about every level of your work, from the narrative as a whole to individual chapters, scenes, and sentences.

o   If you write a whole draft without looking back and don't start revising until it's done, then you've got all the revision to do all at once. This may make facing the revision more daunting because you're looking at rewriting days or months of previous work. Still, forging ahead without having to worry every day about what you wrote the day before can make writing that first draft easier.

o   If you rewrite each individual section before you proceed to the next one, you'll be revising as you go. This approach may make the revision a little less daunting, but it's no guarantee that when you've reached the end, you still won't have to go back and fix mistakes or even make major changes. Even with this method, you still reach a point where you have to think about everything at once—whether the narrative works as a whole and whether all the individual parts work.

Case Study: Revision

•   *The Lecturer's Tale* is the story of Nelson Humboldt, a failing academic who, in the first chapter of the book, loses his right index finger in a freak accident on the quadrangle of the campus where he teaches. After Nelson's finger is reattached, he discovers that he can make anybody do anything he wants by touching them with that finger. He uses this power to save his own teaching job, and as he becomes more corrupt, to work his way to the top of his university's English department.

- The original opening of this novel reads, in part, as follows:

> Crossing the Quad at noon on a grey Halloween, Nelson Humboldt's finger was severed in a freak accident. Oddly enough, he hadn't been hurrying as he usually did at this time of day, and anyway, Nelson was a tall fellow, standing a full head taller than many of the young people around him. If anyone could see where he was going, it was Nelson Humboldt. ...

> But today Nelson was unusually distracted, and this, he decided later, was the reason for the accident. He had just come from the cramped office of the undergraduate chair of the English department, where Nelson was a lecturer, and just ten minutes before she had told him compassionately but briskly that the department was being forced by budget necessities to terminate his appointment at the end of the semester. ... Nelson had no savings to speak of and no prospects, the job market being what it was, and now he was about to have to no job, and he moved much more slowly than usual through the press on the Quad, still in shock, his mind elsewhere, letting himself be buffeted by the currents and eddies of passing students. The loss of his finger was just the last straw.

- This opening doesn't work on either the micro level of sentences and phrases or the macro level of the narrative as a whole. Many of the sentences are just plain clumsy, and the first paragraph doesn't intrigue the reader or suggest something about the narrative to come. The opening is nothing but exposition—an undramatic summary—and there is no evocative detail.

- In the second-draft version, the bare, unevocative summary of the first version is eliminated, and we begin to get the rudiments of an actual scene between Nelson and the chair of the English department, Victoria Victorinix:

> [Nelson] had just come from the spartan seventh-floor office of Victoria Victorinix, the undergraduate chair of the English department, where Nelson was a visiting adjunct lecturer. Just five minutes before the accident Professor Victorinix had told Nelson politely but coolly that the department was being forced by budget necessities to terminate his appointment at the end of the semester. Professor Victorinix was a small, slender, steely woman, with cropped, silvery hair, a penetrating gaze, and the trace of a bemused smile always about her mouth. Nelson appreciated her forthrightness, and the fact that she looked at him as she sacked him; indeed, it was Nelson's glance that roamed all over the white walls and spare, elegant shelves of her office, as he swallowed hard and tried not to cry. The emotion would have been an honest response on Nelson's part, but tears wouldn't have changed anything: Professor Victorinix had suffered twenty-five years of a being ignored, condescended to, and worse as a gay woman in academia, and she was unusually immune to the self-pity of wounded young men.

> "You have our gratitude, of course," she said, "for all your efforts on behalf of the department. Though I realize that under the circumstances, that may not mean much to you."

- The second version is better because it is dramatic and because it starts to show rather than tell. This opening puts the reader in the middle of a situation, providing just enough information to make it intriguing and to suggest what's coming without giving everything away. Not only does the new version work better on the macro level of the whole narrative, but it also works better on the micro level of sentences and evocative details.

- During the course of writing *The Lecturer's Tale*, the character of Professor Victorinix changed from a minor character to a major one. She also changed from merely chair of the English department to, possibly, a vampire. These changes forced additional revisions to the opening scene, the final version of which is more evocative, dramatic, and full of physical details:

> Professor Victorinix was a small, slender, thin-lipped woman with cropped, silvery hair, and a bloodless manner barely masked by a disinterested politesse. Even during the day she kept the blinds of her office drawn, and today she sat in the shadows just beyond the direct glare of the lamp. The reflected glow off her desktop emphasized the sharpness of her cheekbones, the deep groove between her eyebrows, the smooth skullcap curve of her forehead. She regarded Nelson with a gaze that seemed to him aristocratic, ancient, bored.

> "Under the circumstances," she said, "I realize that our gratitude may not mean much to you."

- The additional details here reinforce the fact that Victorinix is powerful and a bit menacing and that she will be important later on. And the use of Nelson's point of view in the opening reinforces the fact that he's the main character of the book.

- Notice that these revisions serve every level of the book. The larger narrative is served by introducing Nelson's point of view and by providing a more vivid and memorable introduction to Professor Victorinix. The chapter is served by starting with a brief description of the accident, then backtracking to show a bit of what happened just before it. The scene is served by providing more action and dialogue to evoke the situation rather than just describing it. And the prose is served by making the sentences clearer and more dynamic.

Lessons Learned

- As these revisions show, some writers work from the general to the specific. Early drafts may be a kind of summary, without much detail and with more exposition than drama. If you find that's the case with your work, when you're revising, ask yourself: What would readers want from this passage that I'm not giving them? What does the character look like or sound like? Where does the scene take place, and what exactly happens in it?

- The key here is to be your own toughest critic. Consider all the techniques we've looked at in this course—evoking rather than describing, using setting to create mood, creating character through detail, advancing the plot through dialogue, and so on—and apply them to your draft.

- If you're interested in lean prose, another technique you might try is to see how much you can cut out of a paragraph or a sentence without altering its meaning or intent. For example, see if you can get an eight-line paragraph down to two lines. This "Twitter technique" of revision is a useful exercise to prevent passages from inducing boredom.

- Other methods you can try include printing the previous day's work and editing it by hand or reading sections or chapters out loud. Reading your work aloud slows you down, so you're more likely to catch grammatical errors and repeated words. It's also a great way to gauge the rhythm and flow of your sentences and decide where paragraph breaks should be. By hearing the words spoken, you catch many missteps that might otherwise slip by you.

Suggested Reading

Ellroy, *L.A. Confidential*.

Gardner, *The Art of Fiction*.

Hynes, *The Lecturer's Tale*.

———, *Publish and Perish*.

1. Reverse the process of writing and revising that you used in the last lecture. If you dashed out something without looking back, sit down with it again and try to fix whatever you think is wrong with it by using some of the techniques in this lecture. If did your revisions as you wrote, try adding something new to the scene—insert a new character, say, or change the setting, or even change the point of view or verb tense.

Approaches to Researching Fiction
Lecture 23

T he amount of research required for a work of fiction depends on the sort of story you're telling. If your story is about a police detective who falls in love, then you might be able to get away with parroting a bit of cop slang to establish your character's identity. But if your story is about the detective investigating a murder, then you need to learn enough about police work to make the character seem realistic. To put it simply, the more research matters to your narrative, the more research you have to do. As we'll see in this lecture, it's also important to strike a balance between factual accuracy and the exercise of your imagination.

Varying Approaches to Research

- One pitfall of writing a story that requires research is that the research sometimes overwhelms the story; in those cases, writers lean too hard on the research and not enough on their imaginations. In fact, the necessity of being completely faithful to the facts is not universally accepted among all writers. Two contemporary writers who personify differing opinions on this issue are Hilary Mantel and Jim Crace.

- Mantel is best known for her historical novels about Thomas Cromwell, who was a Lord Chancellor of the Tudor king Henry VIII. The first two books, *Wolf Hall* and *Bring up the Bodies*, each won the Man Booker Prize, and Mantel has often talked about how much research went into them. In more than one interview, she has stated that historical novelists have a moral responsibility to get their facts straight.

- Jim Crace is another celebrated British author whose novels are often set in the distant past, yet Crace declines to call such books as *The Gift of Stones* (set in prehistoric Britain) and *Quarantine* (about Christ's 40 days in the wilderness) historical novels. He prefers to think of each of them as being set in a sort of alternative, imaginative world.
  - Crace does some research for his books, but he makes up many of the details. In part, this is because he's not interested in the

actual history so much as he is in using a particular historical period as a metaphor for contemporary concerns. The impulse behind *The Gift of Stones*, for example, was the industrial decline of the British city of Birmingham.

o If you read *The Gift of Stones* without knowing that it was originally intended to be a metaphor for the decline of British manufacturing, it reads as a powerful account of an ancient, alien way of life. Whether it's historically accurate is more or less irrelevant to the literary merit of the book or to the truths the book speaks about human nature and the effects of technological change on everyday life.

o Rather than relying on exhaustive research to underpin his narratives, Crace pays close attention to his language, using careful word choices to construct fictional details that seem utterly convincing even if they aren't as scrupulously researched as the details in Mantel's books. In fact, Crace insisted in an interview that if you pick the right words, you don't need to get the facts right. For him, a simple bit of vocabulary can make a fictional world come alive.

• There's an obvious difference in intent between Crace and Mantel. Crace doesn't claim that his novels are accurate; in fact, he tries to subvert the idea of accuracy in fiction and insist on the primacy of storytelling. For Mantel, fidelity to what actually happened matters a great deal.

o It's also true, however, that Mantel is not slavishly dedicated to absolute historical accuracy in all instances. Shrewdly, she has her characters speak in a modern-sounding idiom that makes them seem real to 21st-century readers without also making them sound anachronistic.

o The research Mantel did for *Wolf Hall* is evident on nearly every page, but what makes the novel soar is the way her imagination inhabits the mind of Thomas Cromwell and the way her muscular and modern prose evokes his world.

○ In contrast, Crace's novel *Harvest* is set in the same period of English history as Mantel's novels, but Crace never mentions the year, nor does he include any reference to real historical figures or situations. Instead, he provides a detailed and intimate account of village life. His work has a contemporary immediacy, but Crace evokes the feeling of a distant time and place mainly by using bits of archaic vocabulary.

A Middle Ground

• *Gerontius* is a work by another British novelist, James Hamilton-Paterson, loosely based on the life of the composer Sir Edward Elgar. In the author's note at the beginning of the book, Hamilton-Paterson talks briefly about his research for the book, explaining that he deliberately changed some of the details of Elgar's life, and at the end of the note, he says, "For the rest, I tried to be as factually correct as was interesting."

• This improvisatory, ad hoc attitude to using research seems a sensible approach because it puts the story first. As Gardner said, the primary purpose of a work of fiction is to create a vivid and continuous dream in the mind of the reader, and the two main requirements of any fictional narrative are to be both believable and interesting.

Even the most mainstream novel may often require a few hours of research so that the writer doesn't distract the reader with unnecessary errors of fact.

○ For this reason, it's important to get the facts right because doing so will make the narrative more interesting and believable. At the very least, you don't want to distract the reader with obvious, easily preventable mistakes. If your reader must stop to think about something that doesn't seem right, you've broken the surface tension of the dream.

- o At the same time, you don't want to be boring. Even Mantel has warned aspiring historical novelists not to inundate the reader with everything you've learned. "Don't show off," she says. "Your reader only needs to know about one tenth of what you know. Depth of knowledge gives the writer confidence and suppleness, but doesn't need to be demonstrated on every page."

- Knowing when to back off from the research is also important to the process of writing itself. A work may be backed by extensive research, but it still needs vividly imagined scenes and character. If it is filled only with useless detail at the expense of the story, it will be monumentally dull.

- If you're writing a research-intensive narrative, the research and the writing should be inseparable. In practice, this means that you need to do the writing and the research at the same time, and this, in turn, means that to begin with, you will be writing scenes without having much of an idea of what you're talking about.

Case Study: Using Research Productively
- Let's consider a scene from an incomplete and unpublished historical novel about an 18th-century Dutch explorer named Jacob Roggeveen, who was the European discoverer of Easter Island. In this scene, Jacob travels from his home in the small Dutch city of Middelburg to the much larger and more cosmopolitan city of Amsterdam, where he hoped to win financial support for his expedition to the South Pacific from the Dutch West India Company.

- Early research revealed that Jacob was a notary, which was a kind of lawyer; that he had never married or had children; and that he was a member of a heretical Calvinist sect. Other than that, the first draft of the scene was written without much research into what Amsterdam was like at the time of Jacob's visit. After the rough version of the scene was written, the additional facts that needed to be researched became clear: What would Jacob have seen and heard in the streets of Amsterdam in the year 1719, and how would his fringe religious beliefs have affected his reaction to the vibrant street life of a large city?

- The answers to these and other questions made the scene come alive in the final version.
  - o For example, one important discovery was that the headquarters building of the Dutch West India Company was just off a street near the docks called Haarlemmerstraat. The street was mostly lined with taverns and brothels that catered to sailors.

  - o Another important finding was that the members of Jacob's religious sect did not believe in the idea of sin in the traditional sense. Instead, they saw what others called sinful behavior as ignorance of humanity's oneness with God, who controlled everything people did.

- Here's an excerpt from the scene that attempts to capture what Jacob might have seen and heard on a night in Amsterdam in 1719 and how he might have reacted to it:

  > After a meal of bread and cheese and beer in the smoky kitchen of the inn, Jacob ascended to his hot, airless room up under the eaves. The little window in his room was high—he had to stand to see out of it—and he pushed it open and looked down the steep slope of the roof. Twilight filled the square below, punctuated by fans of lamplight falling out of tavern doorways. He took off his shoes and his waistcoat and tried to sleep on the swaybacked bed, but he only tossed and turned in the breathless heat, kept awake by the nightly riot below. Woven through the roar of the crowd were the whine of fiddles and the wheeze of hurdy gurdys, playing songs Jacob remembered from childhood, rollicking dance tunes accompanied by the clatter of boots against cobbles as sailors and whores danced in the square. Sudden, violent squalls rose above the general racket: the harsh voices of drunken men braying the words of "The Cuckoo's Nest." The shattering screams of women dissolving into cackling laughter. Bottles breaking. The wordless shouting of men in a fight, the loser's howl as a blade pierced him. More cackling laughter. And as the racket finally receded near dawn into a lone sailor singing

tunelessly to himself as he staggered along, Jacob heard carnal groans coming from an entryway just below his window. It was all what his mother used to call wickedness, but Jacob, in his sweaty clothes and tangled sheets, struggled to convince himself that there was no such thing as sin, only ignorance and error, that the poor souls cutting each other in the street or rutting in the doorway were simply stuck in their own flesh like ships run aground in the mud.

- This scene worked because research and imagination played off each other powerfully. Research revealed what a night in the Haarlemmerstraat would have been like, and imagination enabled that experience to be filtered through the consciousness of a single character.

- In the end, the lesson to learn from this case study is that you need to put the story and the characters first. Using your imagination is every bit as important as getting your facts straight. Indeed, we might say that research is just another tool in the service of the imagination. It serves the same function in fiction that plotting, character, and dialogue do: It helps to suggest, to evoke, to put readers in a time and place they might otherwise never experience.

Suggested Reading

Crace, "The Art of Fiction No. 179."

———, *The Gift of Stones.*

———, *Harvest.*

———, *Quarantine.*

Hamilton-Paterson, *Gerontius.*

MacFarquhar, "The Dead Are Real."

Mantel, *Bring up the Bodies.*

———, "Hilary Mantel on Teaching a Historical Fiction Masterclass."

————, *Wolf Hall.*

Wilson, "*Bring up the Bodies* by Hilary Mantel."

Writing Exercise

1. Pick a historical character who interests you, such as Abraham Lincoln or Margaret Thatcher, and write just a single scene about that person doing something ordinary and private, such as playing with his or her children or fixing something to eat, but at an important historical moment. Abraham Lincoln might be thinking about the Emancipation Proclamation, for example, as he plays checkers with his son, or Margaret Thatcher might be making herself a pot of tea late one night at the start of the Falklands War. Try to make the scene personal and intimate without letting the historical events dominate. Remember that research serves the same function in fiction that plotting, character, and dialogue do: to suggest, to evoke, to put readers in a time and place they might otherwise never experience.

Making a Life as a Fiction Writer
Lecture 24

If you want to be a fiction writer, especially a published fiction writer, you need to learn to be two different people. One is the artist, the blinkered and driven obsessive who creates the work in the first place. By necessity, you must be solitary and self-critical, but you may also be moody, self-involved, and distracted. The other is the businessperson, whose responsibility it is to market and sell the work after it has been created. In this role, you need to be confident, good-humored, and gregarious. In other words, you need to be both the lonely genius in a garret and the glad-handing salesperson. In this final lecture, we'll explore these two halves of a writer's life.

The Business of Writing
- Aspiring writers usually want to know two things from published writers: (1) How do I get published, and (2) how do I make a living as a fiction writer? The answer to the second question is: You probably won't. Most writers have to earn a living doing something else and make time to write when they can. To put it bluntly, unless you're a very lucky fiction writer, you shouldn't quit your day job.

- The answer to the first question—how do I get published?—has always been difficult, but it used to be a fairly straightforward process. A writer either got the attention of an agent or a publisher or paid a vanity press to publish his or her work.
   - Many writers sold a story to a literary or genre magazine, which might lead to interest from an agent or a book publisher.

   - Some writers might find their own agents, who would market their work to commercial publishers in New York. The publisher would buy a writer's book and pay an advance against royalties, out of which the agent would take 10 or 15 percent. Then, the writer would go through the process of editing, copyediting, and printing, and between eight months and a year later, the book would come out.

○ Depending on how much money the publisher paid for the book, the writer might be sent on a tour of bookstores, and a publicist might arrange interviews. Lucky writers might have their work reviewed in newspapers and magazines. Most published writers, however, were lucky if they sold enough copies to earn back their advances, which meant that publishers would at least take a look at their next books.

○ There were a handful of writers who got rich off their books and a slightly larger handful, mostly writers of genre fiction, who were able to live off their royalties, but the vast majority of writers considered themselves lucky to be in print, to make a little money on the side, and to be able to write fiction while holding down a day job.

- This process is still the main way that many writers get published, and it's still the way most writers would probably prefer to be published. But in the past 30 years, the publishing industry has gone through enormous changes.

    ○ First, there are essentially only five large commercial publishers of English-language fiction, each of which is only one division of a much larger corporation. These publishers are looking for market blockbusters that will appeal to a large and diverse readership or books that can be marketed to a particular niche. The *midlist writers* today earn smaller advances and get less attention from editors or do not get published at all.

    ○ Second, there are now a large number of small, independent presses that publish the authors the Big Five are no longer willing to publish or promote. These don't pay much, and their books don't usually get much attention from the mainstream press, but their editors devote much more attention to the books they publish, they treat their authors with respect, and they are more likely to keep the books in print for a longer time.

    ○ The third change—and the one that has driven the first two—is the rise of the Internet, the digital revolution, and the success of online retailers. These factors have irrevocably changed the way books are published, marketed, reviewed, purchased, and read.

The New Order versus the Old

- As a result of these changes—the corporatization of commercial publishing, the rise of online bookselling and the e-book, and the consequent decline of brick-and-mortar bookstores—the traditional agents and publishers don't have nearly as much power as they used to.

  o Today, there are essentially no barriers to getting published; anyone with a broadband connection can publish a manuscript online through any number of self-publishing platforms, and for a little more money, a writer can even provide readers with physical books through print-on-demand services.

  o Self-publishing is much more widely accepted, even by authors who have previously published in the traditional way. In certain genres, such as romance fiction, for example, many writers sell their work via the Internet directly to readers, who can download e-books in the space of a minute or two.

- There are also downsides to this new, more democratic order. The main drawback is that getting the attention of readers can be difficult. Breaking into the traditional system is hard, but once you're in, you can at least count on your publisher to send out review copies and possibly even to arrange interviews and appearances. Further, most readers understand that a traditionally published book has at least been edited for spelling and grammar. Self-published writers have to do all their own editing, proofreading, design, marketing, and publicity, or they have to pay people to perform these services.

- On the whole, it seems that the odds of success in the new system aren't all that different from the odds of success in the traditional system. The midlist writer who publishes in the traditional way is not likely to get much more attention than someone who self-publishes an e-book. In both the old and new orders, there are a handful of very successful authors; a large number who sell books only to their friends and loved ones; and a group of midlisters, who write the best books they can, do something else to make a living, and promote their work through social media.

Marketing Your Work

- As much as possible, you should write what you want to write—without trying to tailor your work to appeal to the market—and try to keep business out of the creative process. At the same time, the glad-handing salesperson in you should at least be thinking about how to market your book to the public even as you're working on it.

Professionalism and networking are the keys to attracting the attention of agents and editors or readers in an online community.

- If you plan to publish by the traditional route, do research online to find agents who have worked with writers you admire and publishers that have published the sort of work you're trying to write. If you plan to self-publish, become part of an online community of writers and readers who enjoy reading the sort of thing you're writing.

- The key to attracting the attention of agents and editors or an online community of readers is to be professional. If you approach an agent, for example, write a brief cover letter pitching your novel and say a few words about yourself that make you sound knowledgeable and easy to work with. Mention any previous publications or awards you have received. In an online environment, be respectful, friendly, and brief. Praise the work of others that you genuinely admire and be honest but polite about work you don't like.

Why Write Fiction?

- In 1946, George Orwell published an essay, "Why I Write," in which he listed his four reasons: (1) sheer egoism, (2) aesthetic enthusiasm, (3) historical impulse, and (4) political purpose.

- The first two of these reasons probably hold true for most writers. No writer can function without ambition, but most would likely admit that egoism can be dangerous. Aesthetic enthusiasm is a much more benign and honorable motivation and probably also drives most writers.

- Akin to Orwell's "historical impulse" as a reason for writing is intellectual curiosity about a particular topic or even curiosity about one's own life. A novel is a way of thinking out loud to help writers understand certain issues or to explain their own lives to themselves.
    - As we've seen throughout this course, fiction writing can show you the unmediated consciousness of another person, revealing, as E. M. Forster put it, "the hidden life at its source."

    - This is an essential motivation for all fiction writers, but like any other motivation, it comes with consequences. One is the risk of narcissism, the temptation to believe that everything in your life is as interesting to a reader as it might be to you. The other is the hurt it might cause your family and friends.

- One final reason to write is to erase oneself in the creative act. Writers are achingly self-conscious creatures, and our live-wire awareness of everything around us and the constant hum of our own imaginations cause us to crave some sort of peace. Writing itself is an intensely self-conscious act, as you find yourself inhabiting the minds of your characters and forcing yourself to think about things that most people never think about at all. The paradox is that most writers find respite from this acute self-consciousness in the act of writing itself.
    - This motivation is tied to the desire to re-create the pleasure you gain by reading books you admire, a pleasure that takes you completely out of your own experience or even out of your own self-awareness. This is not the same thing as reading for escape, where your mind switches off and lets the narrative play

as if on a screen. Rather, it's the experience of fully inhabiting another life or world, where your mind is fully engaged—but not as yourself.

o Another way to express this reason is to say that the most sublime experience in writing comes when you feel as if you are remembering the book, not creating it. It is as if the book is out there in the ether someplace, and you are simply recording what you have heard. When you're finished, you feel relief that what's on the page at last matches the melody in your head, the one only you can hear.

• For Orwell, the motive he valued above all others was politics; for many writers, it's more personal. What it might be for you is something only you can find out for yourself. But whatever your motivation turns out to be and whatever struggles and triumphs you have with writing and publishing, the act of creation itself will provide a great deal of meaning and satisfaction in your life.

Suggested Reading

Lamott, *Bird by Bird*.

Orwell, "Why I Write."

Woolf, *A Room of One's Own*.

Appendix: Punctuating Dialogue

Most of what you need to know about the mechanics of writing dialogue can be summed up in a few rules. The vast majority of fiction published since the 18th century has followed these rules, although some great writers, including William Faulkner and Cormac McCarthy, have violated them. In the following paragraphs, Mr. Faulkner and Mr. McCarthy will help us review dialogue rules.

The first rule is that all direct quotations, namely, the exact words of a character, should be set apart from the rest of the text by quotation marks. The second rule is that every time a new character speaks or the speaker changes, his or her first line of dialogue should be set apart with a paragraph break. Also, the first word of a direct quotation always starts with a capital letter. Here's an example that illustrates these rules:

> **"D**o you think quotation marks are necessary?" asked Mr. Faulkner. "Some people say yes; some people say no."
>
> **"I** don't use quotation marks myself," said Mr. McCarthy. "I think they just clutter up a page."

Remember that these rules of punctuation serve two purposes: to set dialogue apart from the rest of the narrative and to identify who is speaking at any given time. The quotation marks and the paragraph breaks serve the first purpose, and the second purpose is served by identifying each speaker with a *dialogue tag*, which in its most basic form is simply the name of the character or a pronoun standing in for the name plus some variation on the verb *said*. In the exchange above, *asked Mr. Faulkner* and *said Mr. McCarthy* are dialogue tags; other common tags include *he said, she said, he replied, she shouted*, and so on.

The rules for punctuating dialogue tags get a little tricky. The first rule is that the dialogue tag is not part of the actual quotation; thus, it should never be included within the quotation marks. The following example is incorrect:

"Do you think this fellow Hynes, said Mr. McCarthy, has any idea what he's talking about?"

The reason it's incorrect is that there are only two sets of quotation marks, one at the beginning of the quotation and one at the end, when there should be four sets of quotation marks: one at the beginning, a second one just before the dialogue tag, a third one right after the dialogue tag, and a fourth at the end, as shown below:

"Do you think this fellow Hynes," said Mr. McCarthy, "has any idea what he's talking about?"

Sometimes a dialogue tag comes in the middle of the quoted sentence; in those cases, the first half of the quotation is set off by a comma and a quotation mark, the dialogue tag is followed by a comma, and the second half of the sentence begins with a quotation mark and a lowercase letter, as shown below:

"I have a feeling," said Mr. Faulkner, "that this fellow Hynes is not paying any attention to us."

However, if a dialogue tag appears between two *complete* sentences, then it is followed by a period, and the second sentence starts with a capital letter:

"There's no reason for him to listen to us," said Mr. McCarthy. "You've been dead for fifty years, and I'm famously reclusive."

There are a couple of additional rules for dialogue: Punctuation always appears inside the quotation marks, and when the dialogue tag appears after the quotation or after the first half of the quotation, the quote can be separated from the tag with a comma, a question mark, or an exclamation point but never with a period. Thus, the following quotations are punctuated correctly:

"That's no excuse," said Mr. Faulkner.

"What can you do with a young fellow like that?" said Mr. McCarthy.

"Kids today!" said Mr. Faulkner.

But the one below is not:

"As far as I'm concerned, there are no rules in creative writing." said Mr. McCarthy.

Let's look at the whole dialogue, this time, punctuated correctly:

"Do you think quotation marks are necessary?" asked Mr. Faulkner. "Some people say yes; some people say no."

"I don't use quotation marks myself," said Mr. McCarthy. "I think they just clutter up a page."

"Do you think this fellow Hynes," said Mr. McCarthy, "has any idea what he's talking about?"

"I have a feeling," said Mr. Faulkner, "that this fellow Hynes is not paying any attention to us."

"There's no reason for him to listen to us," said Mr. McCarthy. "You've been dead for fifty years, and I'm famously reclusive."

"That's no excuse," said Mr. Faulkner.

"What can you do with a young fellow like that?" said Mr. McCarthy.

"Kids today!" said Mr. Faulkner.

"As far as I'm concerned, there are no rules in creative writing," said Mr. McCarthy.

Remember, any good grammar guide will explain these rules in more detail, but an even better way to learn them is simply to model what you do after what your favorite writer does—assuming your favorite writer isn't Cormac McCarthy.

Bibliography

Ackroyd, Peter. *Dickens*. New York: HarperCollins, 1990.

Alvarez, Julia. *How the Garcia Girls Lost Their Accents*. London: Bloomsbury, 2004.

Aristotle. *Poetics*. Translated by Malcolm Heath. London: Penguin Books, 1996.

Atkinson, Kate. *Life after Life*. New York: Little, Brown, 2013.

Austen, Jane. *Emma*. Oxford: Oxford University Press, 1971.

———. *Pride and Prejudice*. London: Penguin Books, 1996.

Baldwin, James. *Giovanni's Room*. New York: Penguin Books, 2001.

Banville, John. *Doctor Copernicus*. New York: Vintage, 1993.

Barker, Nicola. *Darkmans*. New York: Harper, 2007.

Barker, Pat. *The Eye in the Door*. New York: Plume, 1995.

———. *The Ghost Road*. New York: Plume, 1996.

———. *Regeneration*. New York: Plume, 1993.

Bellow, Saul. *The Adventures of Augie March*. New York: Penguin Books, 1999.

Beowulf. Translated by Seamus Heaney. New York: Farrar, Straus and Giroux, 2000.

Berger, Thomas. *Little Big Man*. New York: Dial Press, 1989.

Bernays, Anne, and Pamela Painter. *What If? Writing Exercises for Fiction Writers*. 3rd ed. New York: Longman, 2009.

Borges, Jorge Luis. "Epilogue." In *Dreamtigers*. Translated by Mildred Boyer and Harold Morland. Austin, TX: University of Texas Press, 1964.

Boylan, Roger. *Killoyle*. Normal, IL: Dalkey Archive, 1997.

Brontë, Charlotte. *Jane Eyre*. London: Penguin Books, 2006.

Burroway, Janet. *Writing Fiction: A Guide to Narrative Craft*. 7th ed. New York: Pearson Longman, 2007.

Byatt, A. S. *Possession*. New York: Vintage Books, 1991.

Catton, Eleanor. *The Luminaries*. New York: Little, Brown, 2013.

Chandler, Raymond. *The Big Sleep*. New York: Vintage Books, 1988.

———. *The Long Goodbye*. New York: Vintage Books, 1988.

Chekhov, Anton. "The Darling." In *The Darling and Other Stories*. Translated by Constance Garnett. New York: The Ecco Press, 1984.

———. "The Kiss." In *The Party and Other Stories*. Translated by Constance Garnett. New York: The Ecco Press, 1984.

Chopin, Kate. *The Awakening*. In *Complete Novels and Stories*. New York: Library of America, 2002.

Christensen, Kate. *The Epicure's Lament*. New York: Anchor Books, 2005.

Conan Doyle, Arthur. *The Hound of the Baskervilles*. New York: Barnes and Noble, 2009.

Conrad, Joseph. *Lord Jim*. London: Penguin Books, 2000.

————. *Nostromo*. Oxford: Oxford University Press, 2007.

Crace, Jim. "The Art of Fiction No. 179." *The Paris Review*. http://www.theparisreview.org/interviews/122/the-art-of-fiction-no-179-jim-crace.

————. *The Gift of Stones*. New York: The Ecco Press, 1988.

————. *Harvest*. New York: Vintage Books, 2013.

————. *Quarantine*. New York: Picador, 1998.

Dickens, Charles. *Bleak House*. London: Penguin Books, 2003.

————. *David Copperfield*. London: Penguin Books, 2004.

————. *Great Expectations*. London: Penguin Books, 2002.

————. *Oliver Twist*. London: Penguin Books, 2003.

Dreiser, Theodore. *Sister Carrie*. New York: Penguin Books, 1994.

Egan, Jennifer. *A Visit from the Goon Squad*. New York: Anchor, 2011.

Eliot, George. *Middlemarch*. London: Penguin Books, 1994.

Ellroy, James. *L.A. Confidential*. New York: Grand Central, 1990.

Farrell, J. G. *Troubles*. New York: NYRB Classics, 2002.

Faulkner, William. "A Rose for Emily." In *Collected Stories*. New York: Vintage Books, 1995.

————. *As I Lay Dying*. New York: Vintage Books, 1990.

————. *Light in August*. New York: Vintage Books, 1991.

————. *The Sound and the Fury*. New York: Vintage Books, 1990.

Ferris, Joshua. *Then We Came to the End*. New York: Back Bay Books, 2008.

Fielding, Henry. *The History of Tom Jones, A Foundling*. London: Penguin Books, 2005.

Figes, Eva. *Light: With Monet at Giverny*. London: Pallas Athene, 2007.

Fitzgerald, F. Scott. *The Great Gatsby*. New York: Scribner, 2004.

————. *The Last Tycoon*. New York: Scribner, 1941.

Flaubert, Gustave. *Madame Bovary*. Translated by Geoffrey Wall. London: Penguin Books, 2002.

Forster, E. M. *Aspects of the Novel*. New York: Harcourt Brace Jovanovich, 1955.

Franzen, Jonathan. *The Corrections*. New York: Farrar, Straus and Giroux, 2001.

Gaddis, William. *The Recognitions*. Champaign, IL: Dalkey Archive, 2012.

Gardner, John. *The Art of Fiction: Notes on Craft for Young Writers*. New York: Vintage Books, 1991.

————. *Grendel*. New York: Vintage Books, 1989.

Gibson, William. *Neuromancer*. New York: Ace Books, 1984.

Graves, Robert. *I, Claudius*. New York: Vintage Books, 1989.

Gwynn, Frederick L., and Joseph Blotner. *Faulkner in the University*. Charlottesville, VA: University of Virginia Press, 1959.

Hamid, Mohsin. *The Reluctant Fundamentalist*. New York: Mariner Books, 2008.

Hamilton-Paterson, James. *Gerontius*. New York: Soho Press, 1989.

Hammett, Dashiell. *The Maltese Falcon*. New York: Vintage Books, 1989.

Hawkes, Judith. *Julian's House*. New York: Signet, 2001.

Heller, Joseph. *Catch-22*. New York: Everyman's Library, 1995.

Higgins, George V. *The Friends of Eddie Coyle*. New York: Picador, 2010.

Homer. *The Iliad*. Translated by Robert Fagles. London: Penguin Books, 1990.

———. *The Odyssey*. Translated by Robert Fagles. London: Penguin Books, 1997.

Hornby, Nick. *About a Boy*. New York: Riverhead Books, 1999.

———. *How to Be Good*. New York: Riverhead Books, 2002.

Hurston, Zora Neale. *Their Eyes Were Watching God*. New York: HarperCollins, 2000.

Hynes, James. *Kings of Infinite Space*. New York: St. Martin's Press, 2004.

———. *The Lecturer's Tale*. New York: Picador, 2001.

———. *Next*. New York: Little, Brown, 2011.

———. *Publish and Perish*. New York: Picador, 1998.

———. *The Wild Colonial Boy*. New York: Picador, 1990.

Jackson, Shirley. "The Lottery." In *The Lottery and Other Stories*. New York: Farrar, Straus and Giroux, 2005.

James, Henry. *The Turn of the Screw and The Aspern Papers*. London: Penguin Books, 2003.

James, M. R. "Casting the Runes." In *Count Magnus and Other Ghost Stories*. New York: Penguin Books, 2005.

Joyce, James. "The Dead." In *Dubliners*. London: Penguin Books, 1993.

———. *Ulysses*. New York: Everyman's Library, 1992.

Kafka, Franz. "Metamorphosis." In *Metamorphosis and Other Stories*. Translated by Michael Hoffman. London: Penguin Books, 2007.

King, Stephen. *'Salem's Lot*. New York: Pocket Books, 1999.

Kundera, Milan. *The Unbearable Lightness of Being*. New York: Perennial Classics, 1999.

Lamott, Anne. *Bird by Bird: Some Instructions on Writing and Life*. New York: Anchor Books, 1995.

Le Carré, John. *Tinker, Tailor, Soldier, Spy*. London: Penguin Books, 2011.

Lee, Harper. *To Kill a Mockingbird*. New York: Grand Central Publishing, 1982.

Leonard, Elmore. *Cuba Libre*. New York: William Morrow, 2012.

Lowry, Malcolm. *Under the Volcano*. New York: Harper Perennial Modern Classics, 2007.

MacFarquhar, Larissa. "The Dead Are Real: Hilary Mantel's Imagination." *The New Yorker*, October 12, 2012.

Mansfield, Katherine. "Miss Brill." In *Stories*. New York: Vintage Books, 1991.

Mantel, Hilary. *Bring up the Bodies*. New York: Picador, 2012.

————. "Hilary Mantel on Teaching a Historical Fiction Masterclass." *Fiction at Its Finest*. http://www.themanbookerprize.com/feature/hilary-mantel-teaching-historical-fiction-masterclass.

————. *Wolf Hall*. New York: Picador, 2009.

Marks, John. *Fangland*. New York: Penguin Books, 2007.

Marshall, Paule. *The Chosen Place, the Timeless People*. New York: Vintage Books, 1984.

Martin, George R. R. *A Song of Ice and Fire: A Game of Thrones*, *A Clash of Kings*, *A Storm of Swords*, *A Feast for Crows*, and *A Dance with Dragons*. New York: Bantam Books, 1996, 1999, 2000, 2005, and 2011.

Martin, Valerie. *Mary Reilly*. New York: Vintage Books, 2001.

McCarthy, Cormac. *Blood Meridian*. New York: Vintage Books, 1992.

————. *The Road*. New York: Vintage Books, 2006.

Melville, Herman. *Moby-Dick*. New York: Penguin Books, 2001.

Mina, Denise. *Field of Blood*. New York: Little, Brown, 2005.

Mitchell, Margaret. *Gone with the Wind*. New York: Pocket Books, 2008.

Morrison, Toni. *Beloved*. New York: Vintage Books, 2004.

Munro, Alice. *The Beggar Maid: Stories of Flo and Rose*. New York: Vintage Books, 1991.

————. "Walker Brothers Cowboy." In *Dance of the Happy Shades and Other Stories*. New York: Vintage Books, 1998.

Nabokov, Vladimir. "The Art of Fiction No. 40." *The Paris Review*. http://www.theparisreview.org/interviews/4310/the-art-of-fiction-no-40-vladimir-nabokov.

———. *Lolita*. New York: Vintage Books, 1997.

Némirovsky, Irène. *Suite Française*. Translated by Sandra Smith. New York: Vintage Books, 2007.

O'Connor, Flannery. "A Good Man Is Hard to Find." In *The Complete Stories*. New York: Farrar, Straus and Giroux, 1971.

Orwell, George. "Why I Write." In *Essays*. New York: Everyman's Library, 2002.

Pelecanos, George. *The Cut*. New York: Little, Brown, 2011.

Pinter, Harold. *Betrayal*. London: Faber and Faber, 2013.

Randall, Alice. *The Wind Done Gone*. New York: Mariner Books, 2002.

Rhys, Jean. *Wide Sargasso Sea*. New York: W. W. Norton, 1992.

Robinson, Marilynne. *Housekeeping*. New York: Picador, 1980.

Rowling, J. K. *Harry Potter and the Sorcerer's Stone*. New York: Scholastic, 1997.

Rushdie, Salman. *Midnight's Children*. New York: Random House, 2006.

Russell, Karen. *Sleep Donation*. New York: Atavist Books, 2014.

Schwartz, John Burnham. *Reservation Road*. New York: Vintage Books, 2008.

Sebold, Alice. *The Lovely Bones*. New York: Back Bay Books, 2004.

Shakespeare, William. *Hamlet, Prince of Denmark*. London: Penguin Books, 1970.

———. *King Lear*. London: Penguin Books, 1970.

Smiley, Jane. *A Thousand Acres*. New York: Anchor Books, 2003.

Spencer, Scott. *Endless Love*. New York: The Ecco Press, 2010.

St. Aubyn, Edward. *The Patrick Melrose Novels: Never Mind, Bad News, Some Hope, and Mother's Milk*. New York: Picador, 2012.

Stead, Cristina. *The Man Who Loved Children*. New York: Picador, 2001.

Stevenson, Robert Louis. *Dr. Jekyll and Mr. Hyde and Other Tales of Terror*. London: Penguin Books, 2002.

Stoker, Bram. *Dracula*. New York: Barnes and Noble, 2012.

Stone, Robert. *A Flag for Sunrise*. New York: Vintage Books, 1992.

Sutcliff, Rosemary. *The Eagle of the Ninth*. New York: Farrar, Straus and Giroux, 1999.

———. *The Lantern Bearers*. New York: Farrar, Straus and Giroux, 2010.

———. *The Silver Branch*. New York: Farrar, Straus and Giroux, 2000.

Tolkien, J. R. R. *The Hobbit*. New York: Houghton Mifflin Harcourt, 2012.

———. *The Lord of the Rings*. New York: Mariner Books, 2012.

———. *The Two Towers*. New York: Mariner Books, 2012.

Tolstoy, Leo. *Anna Karenina*. Translated by Richard Peavar and Larissa Volokhonsky. New York: Penguin Books, 2002.

————. *The Death of Ivan Ilyich and Master and Man*. Translated by Ann Pasternak Slater. New York: Modern Library, 2003.

Truffaut, François. *Hitchcock*. New York: Simon and Schuster, 2005.

Twain, Mark. *Adventures of Huckleberry Finn*. London: Penguin Books, 2002.

Updike, John. *Rabbit Angstrom: The Four Novels*. New York: Everyman's Library, 1995.

Wallace, David Foster. *Infinite Jest*. New York: Back Bay Books, 2006.

Welty, Eudora. "Why I Live at the P.O." In *The Collected Stories of Eudora Welty*. New York: Harcourt, 1994.

Wharton, Edith. *The House of Mirth*. London: Penguin Books, 1993.

Whitehead, Colson. *Zone One*. New York: Anchor Books, 2011.

Wilson, Leslie. "*Bring up the Bodies* by Hilary Mantel." *The History Girls*. http://the-history-girls.blogspot.com/2012/05/bring-up-bodies-by-hilary-mantel.html.

Woolf, Virginia. *A Room of One's Own*. New York: Mariner Books, 1989.

————. *Mrs. Dalloway*. New York: Everyman's Library, 1993.

Yourcenar, Marguerite. *The Memoirs of Hadrian*. Translated by Grace Frick. New York: Farrar, Straus and Giroux, 1990.

Zola, Emile. *Germinal*. Translated by Roger Pearson. London: Penguin Books, 2004.

Notes

Notes

Notes

Notes

Notes

Notes